STAGE FRIGHT

Frank, Joe, and Callie hurried down the stairs of the mansion and out the back door. "This way," said Joe, leading them toward the woods.

Just as the three had made it safely to the fence at the edge of the property, Callie stopped suddenly.

"Wait," she said to the Hardys. "Do you hear something—like an animal?"

Frank and Joe held their breath. Now they heard it, too. A baying, like wolves closing in on their prey.

"The Dobermans!" Joe yelled. "The guards must have seen us. They're coming closer!"

Books in THE HARDY BOYS CASEFILES® Series

Available from ARCHWAY Paperbacks

THE HARDY BOYS CASEFILES NO. 19

NIGHTMARE IN ANGEL CITY

FRANKLIN W. DIXON

AN ARCHWAY PAPERBACK
Published by POCKET BOOKS
New York   London   Toronto   Sydney   Tokyo

AN ARCHWAY PAPERBACK *Original*

An Archway Paperback published by
POCKET BOOKS, a division of Simon & Schuster Inc.
1230 Avenue of the Americas, New York, NY 10020

ISBN: 0-671-69185-6

First Archway Paperback printing September 1988

10 9 8 7 6 5 4 3 2

THE HARDY BOYS, AN ARCHWAY PAPERBACK
and colophon are registered trademarks of Simon & Schuster Inc.

THE HARDY BOYS CASEFILES is a trademark
of Simon & Schuster Inc.

Printed in the U.S.A.

IL 7+

NIGHTMARE
IN ANGEL CITY

Chapter

1

"NICE VIEW," JOE HARDY said to his older brother, Frank. "But that first step's a killer."

He turned back to the airplane window. Below him, Los Angeles stretched in all directions as far as he could see. A soft haze hung over the city while, to the west, sailboats rolled on the calm water of the Pacific Ocean and the sun burned huge and bright above the flat horizon. Just then Joe thought it was the most striking place he had ever seen.

Half an hour later Joe and Frank Hardy were traveling in a rented car bumper-to-bumper on the freeway away from Los Angeles International Airport.

"So far it doesn't look like the Los Angeles you see in the movies," Joe said to Frank, who was behind the wheel. Joe peered out at the monotonous row of apartment buildings and shabby bungalows that lined the highway.

"I mean, we're talking Hollywood here," Joe went on. "Where's the glitter? That's what I want to know."

Frank didn't respond to Joe, so Joe let it drop. He knew Frank was worried. But only Joe would be able to detect the signs of strain in Frank's level gaze and see the tension in his lean body as he hunched slightly forward over the wheel.

Frank's dark brown hair had fallen onto his forehead as he concentrated on following the traffic with his eyes. His mind, though, was far away—on his girlfriend, Callie Shaw, to be specific. What trouble was she in, Frank was wondering. He and Joe had just finished a case at their home in Bayport, New York, when Callie called with an S.O.S. from California.

Tired of watching the rear of the car in front of him and disappointed by the roadside sights, Joe scrunched his stocky body up against the door on the passenger side and closed his blue eyes. Joe, seventeen and a year younger than Frank, became drowsy in the hot sun, which was burning into his blond hair.

As Joe drifted off to sleep, he thought back to that morning, when this unexpected case had begun. . . .

* * *

Gertrude Hardy had been sitting at the kitchen table, jokingly wagging her finger at Frank. "You should go out and have some fun," she'd said, more like a command than a suggestion. Their aunt Gertrude had lived with them for years, and throughout Frank and Joe's childhood she'd been like a second mother. "How am I supposed to get any work done with you hanging around the house all the time? This is summer! You're supposed to be off enjoying yourself!"

"I had a double date planned for us with the Basson sisters," Joe said with a sly grin at his brother. "But you know Frank. He has eyes only for Callie."

Frank and Callie had gone together for as long as Joe could remember, and deep down he secretly admired their commitment to each other. But Joe saw no reason to let Frank know that. With a twang he began to sing a country-western song about long-distance love until Frank picked a pillow off the window seat and threw it at him.

"Okay, I know you and Callie will never be best buddies," Frank shot back. "But because she's off on the West Coast taking a course in broadcast journalism doesn't mean I can forget about her. She'll be back in three weeks."

"Right," Aunt Gertrude said. "And I'm sure she wants you to go out and have a good time. I'm not telling you to chase girls with Joe. I just think that you need a break."

3

Aunt Gertrude tended to worry about her nephews, and on the advice of their father—Fenton Hardy, the famous detective—they told her only what they had to about their dangerous exploits.

Frank was relieved when the phone rang and stopped his aunt cold. "I'll get it," Joe shouted, but Frank thrust an arm in his brother's way, cutting him off.

"*I'll* get it," Frank told his brother. The telephone hung on the wall near the kitchen door. Frank lifted the receiver. "Hello," he said. "Hardy residence."

"Frank?" came a distant female voice. "Boy, am I glad you're home!"

He couldn't help smiling as he recognized the voice. "Callie!" he said loudly. "I've been wanting you to call."

"I don't have time to chat, Frank," Callie said bluntly. She sounded breathless and frightened. "Listen. I'm in trouble. I've fallen into some kind of nasty business, and I really need your help."

Frank's expression changed immediately—he was totally focused on the phone call now. "Okay, Callie," he said, scrambling for paper and a pencil. "Tell me exactly where you—"

Before he could finish his sentence, Frank heard Callie cry out. Then her voice was cut off with a clunk!

"Callie!" Frank shouted. She must have

dropped the phone, he told himself. She'd be back in a moment. "Callie!"

"Is something wrong?" Joe asked.

"Quiet," said Frank, cupping a hand over his ear to blot out his brother's voice. Just then a male voice came on the line.

"Who's this?" said the voice.

"Who's *this?*" Frank demanded back. There was a pause, then a click. Frank was listening to a dial tone.

Furious, Frank slammed down the handset. He turned to face Joe and Aunt Gertrude, who both looked startled by his behavior. After he described the phone call, their expressions changed from surprise to worry. "Callie needs us," Frank finished simply.

Joe raised his eyebrows as Aunt Gertrude vanished down the hall. "She's asking us for help? The Callie Shaw I know can take care of herself."

Frank shot an angry glance at him, and the grin fell from Joe's face. "Sorry. But what could have happened to her?"

"That's what I'm going to find out," Frank said, moving toward the door. "You want to come, fine. If not, I'm going anyway."

Joe put a hand on his brother's arm, stopping him. "Hold on, Frank," he said, trying to calm him down. "If you want to fly to Los Angeles, I'm all for it. My only question is, what do we tell Mom and Dad?"

"I'll take care of that," Aunt Gertrude said, reappearing with an overnight bag in each hand. She gave one to each of the boys. "If I know Callie, she wouldn't call for help without a good reason. Go pack, you two. Now."

"Joe," Frank said, nudging his brother with an elbow. "Wake up."

Reluctantly, Joe uncoiled himself and wondered where he was. He looked out the window and remembered they were in California. The road they were on was in shadow as it led up toward the top of a narrow, snaking canyon. "Where are we?" he asked with a yawn.

With one hand on the wheel and one eye on the road, Frank picked up a map of Los Angeles and glanced at it. "Beverly Canyon, in the Santa Monica Mountains," he replied. "Callie's aunt is an actress. She has a house up here, and this is where Callie's staying. I tried to call from Bayport and from the airport, but the phone was always busy." He handed Joe the map. "I wrote the address in the margin. Tell me what it is, okay?"

Joe took the map and found the four numbers. "Yeah, it's 1439." He gazed at the homes they passed. There were no numbers on the doors. Then he realized they were painted on the curbside. "Fourteen twenty-three—thirty-one—there it is."

They pulled into the steep, curved, gravel driveway of a sprawling split-level house, set below the level of the street and nestled back among well-tended bushes and small trees. Joe nodded approvingly. The large redwood-and-brick house was exactly what he had expected to see in California.

After he had parked the car, Frank got out and rang the doorbell.

There was a small click inside, and Frank realized he was being scrutinized through a peephole in the front door. "Who is it?" came a woman's voice.

"Ms. Beaudry? It's Frank Hardy. I'm a friend of Callie's. Maybe she's mentioned me?"

The door swung open. In the doorway stood a beautiful woman with bleached-blond hair. She wore tight blue jeans and a black satin shirt. She looked about thirty years old, but Frank knew she was older. She smiled brightly at Frank.

"She certainly has," Ms. Beaudry said with a grin. She noticed Joe, still sitting in the car. "And that must be Joe!" she added dramatically, bending down to peer into the car.

"That's right," Joe managed to stammer as he got out. He'd expected to meet an aunt, not a California girl.

"Won't you come in?" she asked.

"Thanks, ma'am," Frank said. The boys followed her inside.

7

As she shut the door, Ms. Beaudry said, "Oh, for pete's sake, call me Emma!"

Emma's house was even more pleasant inside than out. Light and airy, it was decorated in pastel pinks and greens, with sliding glass doors offering a beautiful view of the light-filled canyon. Soft rock was playing on a radio somewhere in the house. What trouble could Callie have gotten into here, Frank wondered.

"What can I do for you?" Emma asked. "Would you like a soda? Seltzer? It might be a while before Callie—"

"That's what we came for," Frank interrupted eagerly. "I was hoping we could see Callie."

Emma laughed. "I sure didn't think you came for the seltzer," she said. "Unfortunately, I don't know where Callie is. She hasn't been around in a couple of days." She smiled at Frank's reaction. "Don't look so upset. She's spending a lot of time on a special project for her class, and she said she'd probably stay overnight with a girlfriend sometimes. But I thought she'd call to let me know. When you find her, though, ask her to call me next time. Her mother's my older sister, and she'll kill me if she thinks I'm not being a good chaperon."

"You don't understand," Frank said. "Callie called me and said she was in trouble. She asked us to help. Don't you have any idea where she might be?"

Emma Beaudry's smile faded. "You're kidding," she said worriedly. Without her smile she looked older. "No. She hasn't called or anything. I thought it was strange. She's usually so responsible. Oh, dear, what should I do?"

"There might be something in her room—something to tell us where she's gone." Frank tried to fight a feeling of panic. Now was not the time to get emotional, he told himself sternly. He had one job to do: find Callie, and fast. He noticed Joe giving him a sharp look and quickly rearranged his expression so he looked calm.

"I don't know what could be in there," Emma was saying as she fingered her wooden necklace like a set of worry beads. "But you're welcome to look."

She led them down a hallway to a closed door and swung it open. Inside were two chests of drawers painted hot pink, a brass daybed piled high with pillows, a closet, and a small, white desk. Emma switched on the ceiling light.

"Thanks," Joe said. He eyed the furniture, looking for something out of place, but the room was perfectly neat. "Where do we start?"

"Pick a place," Frank said. As he and Joe stepped across the threshold, the room seemed to explode in a blinding flash of hot white light.

Bits of broken glass from the window danced in the air before they clattered to the floor, and

9

the room filled with heavy, oily smoke. Gasoline! A firebomb!

Joe and Frank stared, caught flat-footed.

Emma Beaudry stood, round-eyed, gazing fixedly into space. "What's happening?" she asked, slowly turning to Joe. Her expression came alive just then, and her mouth fell open. She pointed at Joe.

Frank pivoted and saw flames starting to lick at his brother's shirtsleeve.

"Joe, you're on fire!" he shouted.

Chapter

2

JOE FELL TO the floor and began to roll back and forth on his arm. Still, the flames continued to grow and his skin was being singed.

"Here!" Frank grabbed a blanket from the bed and wound it around Joe's arm.

The blanket did its job—within seconds the fire was out. "You okay?" Frank asked, inspecting Joe's arm.

"Yeah," Joe said stoically. "But we've got other problems. Look around."

Tiny fires had started everywhere around the room—on the drapes, the bed, the area rug—wherever bits of the flaming liquid had landed. Emma scampered from blaze to blaze, trying to smother them with a pillow. But just then the area rug really caught on fire, and flames were rushing up toward the ceiling. "Help me! Please!" Emma yelled.

The brothers sprang into action. "The mattress," shouted Frank. He and Joe grabbed the mattress, their fingers inches from the tongues of fire fanning across it. "Help me flip it," Frank ordered. "If we can bring it down hard over there—"

Joe was already ahead of him. Deftly, he tossed the mattress over, burning side down, on top of the flaming rug. The curtains at the window flared up behind them. Emma tore them down in a heap on the floor. She stamped them out with her sneakers.

Now new fires were springing up, and the walls were starting to burn. Emma ran from the room as the Hardys battled each new blaze.

"No good," Joe called to Frank. "The fire's spreading faster than we can put it out. We'll have to make a run for it."

"Here!" cried Emma from the bedroom door. In her hands was a red metal canister—a fire extinguisher.

"I can't get past the flames," Frank told her, coughing. "You'll have to throw it to me."

Just then the mattress, which had continued smoldering, burst into flame again. This new fire cut Frank off from both Joe and the door. "Throw the canister!" Frank yelled at Emma. "We're going to roast in here!"

Panicked, Emma lifted the extinguisher over her head with both hands and tossed it into the room as hard as she could.

But not far enough, Joe could see. He leapt off the box spring, and, using it as a springboard, dove into the open air as if he were intercepting a pass. He snatched up the fire extinguisher just before it hit the floor, then followed through, landing with a shoulder-roll beside Frank. Joe sprang to his feet and tore the nozzle free from the extinguisher.

White foam smothered the fires. Within minutes the last flame was put out, leaving only greasy smoke lingering in the air.

Frank and Joe staggered out of the room. "Where are you going?" Emma asked as they headed for the door. "What about—"

"No time to explain," Frank said, running past Emma. "Whoever threw that firebomb might have stuck around to see what happened."

"A firebomb? In this neighborhood? You must be kidding!" Emma called after them.

As he threw open the front door, a foot slammed into Frank's chest. It sent him staggering back into Joe, who darted around him and rushed out just in time to see a figure dash around the curve of the driveway, heading up to the street. Joe sprinted up the steep curve after him. But by the time Joe reached street level, the fleeing figure had torn open the door of a red

Porsche parked on the other side of the street and leapt inside.

Even before the car door had slammed shut, the motor roared to life and the Porsche screeched around the corner onto Beverly Glen Drive. Desperately, Joe hurled himself toward the car, but it was too late. The car and the mystery man driving it sped up the twisting road and vanished around a curve.

Joe ran back to the house. Frank and Emma Beaudry were watching anxiously from the top of the driveway. "We can't let him get away!" Joe shouted, racing back to their rented car.

Frank joined him, running down the drive. "Wait a minute, Joe. I'll go. You're hurt."

Joe glowered and looked at his arm. For the first time, he noticed the angry red burns. "You mean these?" he said. "They're no problem."

"Those need some attention. Now!" He opened the car door. "You stay here. *I'll* catch up to our friend. Oh, here's your bag—you need clean clothes," Frank said, tossing out Joe's overnight bag.

Frank climbed into their rental car, then sped out of the driveway and onto the street, turning onto Beverly Glen Drive.

"I should've gone," Joe mumbled, watching his brother roar away. "I should've gone. Did you get a load of that Porsche he was driving?"

Joe asked Emma, who had just joined him. "Whoever we're after has money," he mumbled.

"Or good taste in stolen cars."

Emma Beaudry took his arm and pulled him gently toward the house. "Let's see about those burns. Don't worry about Frank. From what Callie's told me about him, I know he'll be all right."

The canyon road rose higher and higher into the Santa Monica Mountains, twisting and turning more the farther up Frank went.

To his right, the dirt shoulder fell off into a deep gorge. He skidded along a sharp curve, his right tires off the road and on the shoulder. He yanked the steering wheel to the left, sharply edging the tires back onto the pavement.

The road straightened out as it neared the top of the mountain. Ahead, barely visible in the distance, Frank could see a lone red car. He floored the accelerator and roared after it, praying no other car would come onto the road. His speedometer needle moved farther and farther to the right, passing forty, fifty, sixty.

The road straightened and widened into four lanes as at last Frank's car caught up to the car ahead. Frank let out a soft cry of victory.

It *was* the red Porsche.

He slammed on the brakes, his car skidding to the left and swerving around the Porsche. Frank knew he had to cut it off.

The Porsche was jerked to the left, smashing into Frank's car.

He slammed on the brakes again, just getting the car under control before it smashed into an oncoming pickup. The Porsche wove back and forth across the road to keep him from passing.

If that's the way you want to play it, Frank thought, I won't try to pass. But there's no way you're losing me. He stayed on the Porsche's bumper.

They approached a stop sign at the top of the hill. The Porsche sped up, racing through the intersection and around a curve. Frank heard the car screech to a halt around the side of the mountain, its tires squealing wildly.

"Spun out, huh?" Frank muttered as he neared the curve. "Now I've— Huh!"

As he rounded the curve Frank was blinded by the bright sun, shining straight into his eyes. Just ahead of him he saw the blurred shape of the Porsche. It was stopped, and it was facing him.

Frank slammed on his brakes and watched in horror as the Porsche revved up and drove straight at him.

"What the—" Crying out, Frank hit the gas and yanked the wheel hard to the right to avoid the car. But he couldn't make the turn back onto the road and crashed through the guardrail—and off the side of the mountain, flying into space to the canyon floor far below!

Chapter

3

As THE CAR was shearing through the guardrail at the top of the cliff, Frank fumbled for the door handle. Large spots from staring at the sun still swam in front of his eyes, but his sight had returned enough to see the huge San Fernando Valley spread out below him. A weightlessness gripped the car. He was falling into that valley!

Frank rammed his shoulder into the door. His seat belt unbuckled, he took a deep breath and hurled himself into space.

He groped wildly, desperate for any handhold. One miraculous snatch and he did get his fingers around a tree branch. Twisting his body, he fought to grab on with the other hand. He continued dropping for a few seconds, then a shock jolted through his arms as he abruptly stopped. The limb held!

From beneath him came the screams of metal tearing on rock until one huge explosion echoed through the air, and only the crackle of fire broke the welcome silence.

Relaxed by the quiet, Frank began to drift off, his grip on the tree loosening. He shook himself violently. It's shock, he told himself. I have to stay awake. He looked down and saw where he was, dangling from a tree limb over a deep ravine. Pain shooting through his arms and shoulders, he pulled himself up on the branch and lay there for a minute before shinnying down the trunk.

Minutes later he scrambled up the hill to the road. The red Porsche was long gone. With no one in sight he began the lengthy walk to a police station.

I hope Frank's all right, Joe Hardy thought for the thousandth time in several hours. He sat in an easy chair in Emma Beaudry's living room, his burned arm wrapped in cold wet towels. The VCR was on, and Joe was fast-forwarding through videotapes with a remote control. He and Emma had found the tapes in an unburned bureau in Callie's room and decided to look through them for clues. There was nothing suspicious or unusual about them. They appeared to be tapes Callie had made in her broadcast journalism class.

Right then Joe was watching a press conference that had also been filmed by all the major networks. None of the tapes seemed to be a reason for trying to burn down a house.

Callie's aunt appeared, carrying a tray. She set it down and poured each of them a glass of iced tea.

"Ms. Beaudry? Don't you know the names of any of Callie's friends here? Someone we could call?"

"Call me Emma, please," she insisted, smiling wearily. "As I said before, Callie spent all her time working on her class. She didn't bring any of her friends back here. All I know for certain is that she was very excited about her final project. She had to make a short news feature."

"Great," Joe replied. He sipped at his tea. "Nothing else?"

Emma shook her head. "No. The last time I saw her was a couple of days ago. She asked if I had any old clothes I didn't need anymore. I gave some to her, and she left for school."

"Where is that?" Joe asked, glancing at his watch nervously. It was getting late now. He wished he had some way to contact Frank.

"UCLA," Ms. Beaudry replied. "The University of California at Los Angeles. Over in Westwood. It's one of the largest in the country." Joe continued to stare at the television, expression-less. She raised her voice. "Surely you've heard of it?"

"What?" Joe asked. "Sorry. I was distracted. I'm worried about Frank. Listen," he said. "Maybe we should call Callie's parents. They deserve to know that their daughter may be in trouble."

"Please, no!" Emma said, her sophisticated air disappearing. "Really, my sister would *kill* me. Can't you boys handle this? You're hotshot detectives, aren't you? You were so wonderful with the police."

Emma had summoned the Beverly Glen police to witness the damage to her house before she called her insurance company.

Joe frowned. He had no idea who'd want to firebomb Emma's house, or why. He'd kept his suspicions—that the fire had something to do with Callie's absence or that it was a move to destroy evidence or even to scare the Hardys away—to himself. Now Joe wondered if he shouldn't have shared his hunches with the police because he was beginning to think that Frank's life might be at stake. He checked his watch again. Eight o'clock!

The doorbell rang, cutting off Joe's thoughts. "I'll get it," Emma said, jumping up from the couch.

"No, I will," Joe said. They raced together for the door.

On the front porch Frank was standing, his clothes torn and bloody, his face pale with exhaustion. Behind him, a cab backed out of the driveway and drove off.

Joe helped him to a chair. "What happened to you? And where's the car?"

"Don't ask. I just spent an hour at the car rental office trying to convince them and a policeman that our car went over a cliff because I was trying to avoid hitting a dog. They didn't offer me another car," he said flatly, and explained what happened.

"What about the guy you were chasing?" Joe asked.

"He got away. But I did learn something—maybe. I think he was a cop. I got *one* good look at him when he turned around to check me out. I think he was wearing a patrolman's uniform."

Joe looked puzzled. "Why?" he said, asking the question for all of them. After they were seated in the living room, Joe told Frank about the tapes.

"But you found nothing on them?" Frank asked.

"Absolutely nothing," said Joe, shaking his head. "No coded messages, no dangerous news stories—nothing out of the ordinary. There was nothing in Callie's room worth the gasoline for that bomb.''

Frank shook his head. ''Obviously, our attacker *thought* something was here and didn't want us to get it.''

''Like what?'' Emma asked. ''What could Callie be hiding?''

''That's the problem,'' Frank replied. ''The only one who knows is Callie. And if someone is throwing bombs and trying to kill me because of it, she could be in really bad trouble. We *have* to find her. Who else might know where she is?''

''Emma said Callie's been working on a special project at school,'' Joe began. ''So her professor might have some idea. What do you say? Head for UCLA?''

Frank nodded.

''But it's after eight o'clock,'' Emma added. ''None of the offices will be open.''

''A little thing like that won't stop us,'' said Joe. He set his glass down on the tray, and he and Frank started for the door.

''Boys,'' Ms. Beaudry said with a smile. ''UCLA is casual, but I don't think anyone will talk to Frank dressed like that.''

''Maybe you should change,'' Joe said. ''I've got something you can wear.''

''I'll be quick,'' Frank replied grimly.

Emma Beaudry insisted she drive the boys in

her car. "Thanks for everything," Joe said as they all went out.

"Call me the minute you find something," said Emma, walking out to her car. "Callie's sensible, but still—I'll be up all night worrying."

"Will do." Joe grinned reassuringly as he climbed into the passenger seat. "I'm sure you're right, Emma. Callie's probably just out chasing a scoop. We'll call you as soon as we can."

Emma Beaudry gave him a dazzling smile of gratitude and backed out of the drive.

"Look, Frank," Joe said as they trudged along a street through UCLA. The boys had been dropped off blocks earlier because the street was closed to traffic. A few students, carrying armloads of books, walked past them as they came from the direction of the library. "Emma said it was only a couple of miles to UCLA, but she never mentioned the couple of miles we'd have to walk *into* it. This place is the size of a small city."

Frank barely heard him. He was too intent on looking at the buildings. "There it is," he finally said, pointing to a modern building of concrete and glass. School of Journalism was posted on a large sign in front of it.

"Great," said Joe. "What do we do?"

"Callie told me she was studying with a guy named Reese. Let's see if we can find his office."

"And if he's not here?" Joe asked.

Frank shrugged.

They walked up the front steps, and Joe pulled on the door. It opened, and the two entered the apparently deserted building. The first-floor corridor was lined with office doors bearing the names of the occupants. Near the end of the hall Frank found a plaque that read Prof. James Reese, Ph.D. "Here it is," Frank said. He knocked on the door. No answer. He tried to open the door. Locked.

Joe stepped forward and pressed his face against the glass and peered in. "No way we're getting in there tonight." He shook his head slowly.

Not even sure what they had expected to find, the boys walked out of the building feeling unbearably frustrated and dejected. The last bit of light from the setting sun still washed the sky with splashes of pale pink. "How about we go get something to eat and figure out where to sleep tonight?" Joe said, admiring the last of the color.

"I don't know if I can eat. I keep thinking about that call from Callie. We don't even know if she's alive still. We've got to do something— and quick." Frank grew steadily more agitated as he spoke.

"If you don't eat, you'll get sick and won't be able to help anyone—not even yourself," Joe reminded his brother.

Frank smiled and shrugged. "Okay," he said. "Lead on!"

Minutes later they stepped through the south gate of UCLA and onto a street of Westwood. Brightly lit stores lined the street, and the Hardys walked down the block, looking for a restaurant.

Just then a young man bumped into Frank. "Hey, watch it," Frank said, rubbing his arm while he looked at the guy. Despite the heat of the Los Angeles night, he was dressed in several layers of clothing. With fearful eyes he watched Frank as he backed away, disappearing into the night.

"Come on," Frank said, shrugging the encounter off and grabbing Joe by the arm. He pulled him toward a Mexican restaurant. "It is time for some food." He tapped his palm against his pocket with his wallet. He stopped dead in his tracks.

"My wallet. It's gone," he said with a note of disbelief. "That kid picked my pocket."

"You mean *that* kid?" Joe said. The young man was creeping toward an alley.

"Right. Him," Frank replied angrily. He shouted, "Hey, you! Give me back my wallet."

The young man looked up with round, startled eyes and then darted into the alley. The Hardys tore after him but stopped when they entered the alley. The young man was no longer fleeing; he was standing halfway down the concrete canyon, watching them defiantly. Cautiously, they moved forward again.

As their eyes grew accustomed to the darkness of the alley, the brothers gradually picked out shapes moving in some of the darkened doorways. Joe and Frank slowed to a halt as, one by one, the shapes took human form and inched forward to surround them.

Frank clenched his fists. "Get ready," he muttered to Joe. "Looks like we're in for it."

Chapter
4

THE HARDYS PRESSED their backs together. "Take out as many as you can," Frank whispered to Joe, "before we make a break for it." From every direction the menacing figures continued to stalk them. Then suddenly they began to snicker among themselves, until the alley seemed to become filled with laughter.

"Okay, guys, that's enough!" cried a voice.

To the brothers' surprise, the people turned away as they were just an arm's length from the Hardys.

From a doorway stepped a woman. It was too dark to see her face, but in the light from the street the Hardys could see she was dressed in a ragged jacket and blue jeans. Her head, covered by a ski cap, appeared to be too small for her body. Then Joe realized that she, too, was wearing several layers of clothing. In her hands were several bulging shopping bags.

With a quavering voice the woman said, "So you think this poor boy has your wallet?"

Frank blinked and strained his eyes to catch a glimpse of the bag lady's face. Despite the distorted way she had spoken, he knew that voice!

"Callie?" he said cautiously. Everyone broke into uproarious laughter again, and, grinning, Callie Shaw strode into the light.

"Callie Shaw!" Joe snapped angrily. "What are you doing? Frank's been going nuts wondering what's happened to you."

"Nice to see you, too, Joe," Callie said.

The circle of street people stepped aside, and Frank moved close to Callie. "What's going on here? Why are you dressed like that? Who are these people?" Involuntarily, he wrinkled his nose.

"The smell," Callie whispered. "I know. It took me a while to get used to it too." She gestured to the street people and raised her voice. "Everyone, these are my friends, Frank and Joe Hardy. Meet Adrienne, Frank and Joe."

A small woman, barely older than Frank, nodded slightly. She wore blue jeans, a sweatshirt, and old sneakers with the toes worn through. "Pleased to meet you," she said.

"Bob and Jimmy."

Two men—the first black, wearing a short windbreaker and corduroy trousers, and the second, white and bearded—grinned and said, "Howdy."

An older man with cowboy boots and a three-day stubble leaned toward the Hardys. "I'm Charlie," he said. "You can call me Charlie."

Callie flagged forward the boy who had taken Frank's wallet. "Okay, Lewis. You can give Frank his wallet back. Don't worry, he won't hurt you." To Frank and Joe she said, "I needed some way to get you to come to me without showing myself."

The boy called Lewis moved toward them, the wallet stretched out before him. Frank took the billfold as Lewis backed away quickly into the darkness.

Callie watched Frank check the contents of his wallet. "Come on, Frank!" she said, annoyed. "They're not thieves, they're street people."

"We're artists," Bob corrected her. "Just down on our luck."

"You still haven't explained what you're doing here," Joe told Callie.

"Yeah, Callie," Frank said, angry now. "You told me on the phone you were in trouble. We were cut off with a clunk—I thought you might be dead."

"I'm sorry if I scared you. But I really am in trouble. Look, I've got to catch a bus to Santa

29

Monica. That's where we're staying. I'll tell you everything on the way. Will you come?" Frank didn't budge. "Please, I need you."

Frank knew Callie must really be in trouble or she wouldn t have pulled such a rotten stunt. "Okay," he said, and nodded once. "Joe?"

Joe nodded too. "Why a bus?" Joe asked.

"Two reasons," said Callie. "First, it's the only thing, besides walking, my friends can afford. Second, buses stop and go. It's easy to spot someone tailing a bus."

"Tailing?" Frank repeated apprehensively. "What kind of trouble are you in?"

"Like you wouldn't believe. It's a big story. Come on, I'll tell you all about it."

The abandoned bottling plant, decades old, stood on the beach between the Santa Monica pier and new condominiums built to the south. Once the plant had bottled a local brand of soft drink. It would be gone soon to make room for more condominiums, but in the meantime it housed dozens of homeless people, most of them artists or musicians. Many had their musical instruments with them. Others kept supplies of paper and ink for drawing beside their makeshift cots. The walls inside the plant had been painted with vividly colored murals in many different styles.

"There's quite a little art colony here," Callie

told Frank and Joe as they toured the building. "They're great people, but for one reason or another they don't have homes, so they camp out here. They help one another out."

"Wonderful," said Joe, getting angry. "Callie, we flew for six hours. I've been scorched. Frank had to jump from a speeding car. We're both dead tired—we want to know what's going on."

"Okay," Callie said. "You know about my broadcast journalism class."

"Yes," said Frank, not sure if he could believe anything now.

"Well, when I heard about this colony of artists, I decided to do my final class project on them. You know, interview them, tape their daily routines. But when I approached them, they didn't want anything to do with me. I had to get close to them."

"So you pretended to be one of them," Joe observed. "Callie, I didn't think you had it in you."

"Thanks—I think," Callie said. "Anyway, it was great. I had a videocamera concealed in a bag and my microphones hidden in my clothes. They didn't even know the equipment was there. After a day they started talking to me. And I decided to narrow my report down to six people: the five you met and Patch."

"Patch?"

"I don't know what his real name is. He's an

older man—in his forties, I'd say. He has a patch over his right eye, so everyone calls him Patch. Well, I couldn't get him to open up to me.

"So I followed him—discreetly, from a distance. A couple of times he spotted me and ducked away, so I started following him in disguises.

"Last night when I followed him, I tracked him to the beach up near Pacific Palisades. He waited in one spot until about five this morning. Then a policeman came onto the beach—"

"A policeman?" Frank said.

"Yeah. He was in uniform and carrying a briefcase," Callie continued. "I thought it was strange, so I started videotaping the whole thing. They seemed to know each other. Patch started yelling at the cop, but I wasn't close enough to hear what he was saying. The policeman handed Patch the briefcase, and as Patch opened it, the policeman drew his revolver and aimed it at Patch."

"And, of course, you yelled," Joe said, speculating.

"Isn't that what *you* would have done?" Callie said sharply. "This is *my* story. Please stop interrupting. When the policeman heard my voice, he spun around and aimed at me. He was a good shot too. He smashed my camera, and I thought I was done for. But Patch stopped him. He hit him over the head with the briefcase."

She frowned. "It flew open, and I could see it was empty. Whatever the policeman was supposed to bring he didn't. Patch took off down the beach while the policeman staggered in loopy circles. I grabbed the camera and took off. It didn't look like anyone was chasing me, so I stopped at the first phone booth and called you. I thought I'd better get some help."

"Then what?" asked Frank.

"Then, right after we talked a minute, I saw the cop coming down the road toward me. I dropped the phone and ran. Late this afternoon when I got to school I heard a policeman had been nosing around looking for me. How he traced me to school I can't figure."

"But once he found out who you were it must've been easy to learn where you were staying. With Emma," Frank said.

"Aunt Emma? I forgot to call her!" Callie said, covering her mouth with her hand. Now she looked more like the Callie that Frank and Joe remembered. "Has anything happened to her?"

"No," Frank said hesitantly, deciding not to say anything about the firebomb. "She's worried sick about you," Frank said very pointedly.

"Has she called my parents?"

"No, but she'll have to if she doesn't hear from you soon," Joe informed her.

"I'll call her right away," she said. "I haven't

been home for a couple of days," she explained. "When I got in with these people, I felt I had to stay."

"Now, listen, Callie. You've got to go back to Bayport on the next flight out. You're in more danger than you know."

"Frank Hardy!" Callie snapped. "Are you telling me to give up on a case?"

"I'm not telling. I'm asking," Frank replied sternly. "You're very important to me, and I want you out of—"

"Sorry to break you two lovebirds up," said Joe, "but do you smell something funny?"

Frank sniffed. "Gas," he said, surprised. He listened. Beneath the drone of voices he could hear a soft hiss. "Everyone out!" he shouted. "There's a gas leak."

Everyone crawled out of their beds and ran for the main door. "It won't open," one of them shouted. They all beat on it with their hands, then rammed it with their shoulders, but the steel door held.

Joe began to cough and looked up where the windows had once been set. They were boarded up now. "This place is filling up pretty quickly," Joe said, blurting out his words between gasps. "The gas must have been leaking for a while. We have to get out soon—this place is going to blow."

He barely heard his brother say, "It's no good. We're trapped." Joe tried to answer, but he felt suddenly dizzy.

Then Joe Hardy's legs gave out, and he pitched forward into darkness.

Chapter

5

FROM SOMEWHERE JOE heard his brother's voice. "Joe, get up! If you go to sleep, you'll die. Wake up!" He felt a sharp pain in his cheek. Frank had pinched him.

Groggily, Joe opened his eyes. He wanted only to sleep. But he fought the lack of oxygen, and by sheer willpower forced himself to his feet. All around, everyone was scrambling to get out. But the other exit was jammed too. It was no good. Several people had collapsed as Joe had.

Joe's vision blurred as his eyelids started to close again. He shook himself awake. "Put something over your mouth and nose," Frank said. "It'll help filter out the gas." Joe ripped his sleeve from his shirt and tied it around his face.

Frank looked up at the boarded windows a

good fifteen feet above his head. He started to sway on his feet, and Joe could tell the fumes were getting to him too. Callie sat down, and Frank harshly pulled her back to her feet. "Gas is heavier than air," he warned. "Down there you're finished." He stared at the windows again. "Up there I could breathe long enough to figure a way out—maybe."

Joe studied the factory. "The windows are too high up, Frank. Even if we made a pile of everything in this place, we couldn't reach them."

Frank tried both doors again. They didn't budge. "Something's blocking them outside." He gazed at the windows again. "They're our only hope, but how can we reach them?"

Callie brightened. "A human ladder." She ran to the others—the few who were still standing.

Two of the people started forcing their groggier companions to their feet, and soon they were all on their feet and shambling over to the Hardys.

"Here's your ladder," Callie said before coughing.

Bob braced himself against the wall next to Charlie. One man climbed up on Bob and stood with one foot on Bob's shoulders and one on Charlie's. One last man shinnied up to top off the pyramid.

Callie nudged Frank. "Go on."

"Give me your belt, Joe," Frank said, and Joe peeled it off and shoved it into Frank's hand.

Carefully, Frank climbed the human ladder. Everyone was wobbly from the gas. At the top Frank tied Joe's belt to a pipe running beside the windows and looped his arm through it.

"I'm secure," he called down. "Everyone down now. I don't want anyone hurt." Suddenly there was nothing under his feet, and he dangled for a second until he reached up with his free hand to get a grip on the pipe. Below him, the human ladder was collapsing. He had only minutes left before everyone, including Callie and Joe, would be overcome. He had to work fast.

Quickly, he slid off his own belt and wedged the buckle under a plank of wood, hoping to work loose the nails holding the board to the building. Nothing. He pulled harder, but nothing budged. Frantically, he closed his eyes and yanked with all his strength.

The nails held, but the wood, rotted by the sea air, gave way, shattering into splinters. Frank saw the glass on the other side of the wood. Wrapping his belt around his hand, Frank punched through the glass. Cool sea air rushed in to sting his lungs and face.

Gulping the air, his strength returned and he found it easier to break the rotting boards. Within seconds he had cleared an area large enough to crawl through. Reaching the window latch, he slipped the window up, then pulled himself through the opening.

It was a twenty-foot drop to the beach. He dangled at the window's edge for a second, then let go, going limp as he fell. He crumpled as he hit the sand, rolled with the impact, and sprawled to a stop.

Legs aching from the shock, Frank forced himself to his feet and ran to the main door of the bottling plant. Someone had shoved a small dumpster against it and locked the wheels in place so it couldn't be moved. He kicked the locks free and shoved the bin out of the way.

The door swung open and everyone spilled out onto the beach, hungrily gulping the fresh air. Last out were Callie and Joe. Frank joined them on the sand.

"Everyone's out," Callie said. "That policeman must really want to get me. He nearly killed a whole building full of people."

"Hold on," said Frank. "We don't know for sure that our suspect is really a policeman. Second, he wasn't the one who did this."

Both Joe and Callie looked surprised. "What?"

"Think about it. No one followed us here. We were watching, and we'd have spotted him. And if he already knew you were staying here, he would have gone after you *here,* earlier, rather than at your aunt's house."

"Then," Callie began nervously, "someone else might be after me too."

"Right," said Joe. "It'd have to be someone

who knew the plant though. I bet if we check, we'll find a gas pipe that's been broken open. The place filled up too quickly. It couldn't just have been a leak.''

Frank nodded. "The trouble all started when you made that videotape. It's a good bet that's what that policeman was after. Now, who else would know about that videotape?''

Callie could tell by his voice that he wasn't really asking a question.

Joe picked up on Frank's thought. "And would know enough about the bottling plant to turn it into a deathtrap?''

"And would know you were hanging out here?'' Frank continued. "And would want the videotape for his own reasons?''

"Patch?'' Callie said, dismayed. "He's one of the most harmless men I've ever seen. They say he's been around here forever.''

"Obviously, the policeman didn't think he was harmless, or he wouldn't have tried to shoot him,'' said Joe. "So what was supposed to be in the briefcase? What's the connection between Patch and the policeman?''

"I bet that tape shows more than you know,'' Frank told Callie. "I'd like to see it. Where is it?''

Callie chuckled. "You wouldn't believe me if I told you.'' She picked up her bags and began digging through them.

Her grin faded. "No," she mumbled. "Oh, no. It's gone. Someone took it."

"What?" Joe said. "You had the tape on you all this time?"

"Sort of," Callie revealed. "It must have happened inside the plant. Someone must have stolen the tape."

"Terrific," Frank said. "Everyone from inside has scattered now. I think it's time Joe and I had a talk with this Patch. You said he had a shack on the beach. Where?"

"There's a fish restaurant a couple of miles up the coast, where Sunset meets the ocean," Callie said. "Go about a quarter of a mile past that. It's there, hidden behind a boat house." She got to her feet. "Come on. I'll show you."

"No way," said Frank. "You're staying right here."

"I'm coming with you," Callie retorted.

Frank sighed. "Not this time, Callie. You're safer here with your friends. Maybe you can see if one of them knows where the tape went. Plus, there could be trouble. . . ."

Anger raged on Callie's face. "I can take care of myself."

"Under most circumstances, yes," Frank said. "But this Patch could turn out to be a lot more dangerous than you think. I think you should stay here. Come on, Joe." They turned and walked off down the beach without her.

"I won't forget this, Mr. Frank Hardy," she yelled after them. "Just wait till you need *my* help next time!"

A hand tugged on her arm. It was Lewis, looking anxious. "Callie," he began.

"Not now, Lewis. I have to catch up to my friends."

"But, Callie," Lewis insisted. "I got a message from Patch. He wants to see you at the mall right away."

"Patch?" Callie looked at Lewis quizzically, then a smile widened across her face. "Thank you, Lewis. Thank you very much." She smiled triumphantly at the figures of Frank and Joe, already vanishing in the distance. "Now we'll see who's so smart."

Santa Monica Mall at midnight looked like a Hollywood set that had been abandoned but not torn down.

Callie Shaw, decked out in her street costume, walked cautiously through the outdoor mall, looking for signs of life. There were none.

"Kind of quiet here this time of night, isn't it?" said a raspy voice from the shadows.

"Patch?" Callie asked as a hefty man stepped into the light. His shoes didn't match, his clothes were threadbare, and a black patch covered one eye. His hands were in his pockets. Smiling, he stepped very close to Callie, and she backed up against a building. Patch's one eye looked sinister and cold in the blue light.

"I know you, Patch," Callie said, trying not to sound afraid. "I know you'd never hurt me."

"Don't be so sure," he said slowly, drawing his hand from his pocket. With a sharp click a switchblade knife flashed into view. "I've killed before." He sighed loud and long. "And you're next on my list."

With one strong motion he shoved Callie against the wall. She screamed as he raised the knife to her throat.

Chapter

6

"I DON'T THINK I've ever walked so much in my life," Joe Hardy complained. He and his brother were tromping down the beach. Behind them was the fish restaurant, its sign bright against the night sky.

A wave washed onto the beach, soaking Joe's shoes. He splashed out of the surf, but his feet and ankles were already drenched. For the hundredth time he wished he were in a nice warm bed.

"I think that's the shack," said Frank, who was farther up the beach, avoiding the water. Ahead Joe saw an old boat house. It looked as if it hadn't been used in years.

"That's what you said at the last three," Joe

replied. "I don't see the shack Callie was talking about."

"Doesn't matter," said Frank. "It couldn't be anything else. Maybe Callie was wrong about the shack."

"Figures," Joe said. He reached the boat house and rubbed one of the windows clean with his hand. It was dark inside and, as far as he could tell, empty. "I wonder why there's so much abandoned property out here."

"Beats me," Frank answered. The boat house was set on the end of a large pier that stretched far out into the ocean. Like the boat house, it was no longer in use. Many of its planks were missing. Joe was right. There was no shack.

"What are you doing, Frank?" Joe called as Frank walked onto the pier, stepping over the gaps.

"Just a hunch," said Frank. He stared through a hole at the ocean below. White foam and dark water were rushing onto the land, bringing the water level almost to the pier, and then the tide ebbed. What water had covered just moments before was now muddy sand.

"Come down off there," Joe shouted. "Look at it swing. It could give way any second."

Just then Frank disappeared. It seemed that he had dropped through a hole in the floor. Horrified, Joe sprinted onto the pier. His foot crashed through a plank, and the pier split open, dumping him rudely onto the sand ten feet below.

"Nice of you to drop in," said Frank, grinning.

"Oh, you came down here for a look-see?" Joe said angrily. "You could have let me know. I thought you'd broken your leg, falling through like that, and gotten washed out to sea—"

Frank interrupted him. "We will be if we're still here when the tide comes back in. Anyway, I found what we're looking for." He pointed deep under the pier, at the end by the boat house.

Hidden in the shadows at the very end of the pier was a tiny, crude hut cobbled together from odd pieces of wood. It was half soaked, but it was clearly a shack.

"Patch lives there?" said Joe, surprised. "No way. If he slept there, he'd drown."

"Maybe that's the point," Frank said. He walked back to the shack and pushed the door open. Frank and Joe went inside, and paused for a moment to let their eyes get used to the darkness.

The shack was empty except for a shovel and an old pair of shoes on a shelf inches from the ceiling. "Why would he build a shelf way up there?" Joe wondered aloud. "And how does he reach it?" His thoughts were broken by a dull roar.

"The surf," Frank said. "It's coming back in."

"No time to get out," Joe said. "We'll have to ride the wave."

Water slammed into Joe, pushing him to the back wall of the shack and filling his mouth and nose. He pushed himself off the wall and up, fighting the force of the wave. A second later his head bobbed up into the air pocket next to the ceiling.

"Now we know how Patch reaches the shelf," said Frank, who treaded water next to Joe. The water had raised them so Frank could easily reach over and touch the old shoes.

"That's not all," Joe said, looking up. Light crept through the cracks in the ceiling. "We must be right under the boat house." Propping himself against the shelf, he shoved at the ceiling. It gave way.

Straining against the weight of their water-logged clothes, the Hardys pulled themselves up through the trapdoor and into the boat house. Light moved across the boat house and disappeared, thrown by headlights of cars passing on the nearby highway.

"This Patch is no dummy," Joe said. "He really does live in the boat house, but the only way in, without breaking through the padlocked door, is through the shack at high tide. Pretty clever." In a corner of the boat house was a small bed made of newspapers. Other than that, there was no sign that anyone had been there. Joe looked at Frank, who stretched his arm down through the door. "What are you doing?"

Frank was holding the shoes that had been on the shelf. "Just seeing what's so important about these." He reached inside them. "That's odd. The toes are stuffed with scraps of newspaper."

"Maybe he wants to hold their shape."

"Maybe," Frank agreed. "But inside them are airtight plastic bags with more newspaper inside *them*."

They tore open the bags and took the clippings out, spreading them on the boat house floor. They read them in the flashes of light provided by the passing cars. "These are all ten years old," Joe realized. "And they're all about the same thing."

Frank raised one of the clippings so it would get as much light as possible and squinted at the print. "According to this, there was an armored car heist in Philadelphia back then. Two masked and armed robbers dropped from a highway overpass onto the truck, forced the driver to pull over, overpowered the guard, and walked off with two million dollars."

"Walked off with it? On foot? That's a lot of money to carry."

Frank nodded. "It says they escaped on foot through a drainage tunnel."

"So they got away?"

"Not quite. *One* of them did." Frank rubbed his eyes and waited for another car to pass. "The police sent dogs out after them. After two days one of their bodies was found near the Delaware

48

River. It had been burned, but could be identified as a professional robber named Sam Moran."

"What about the other one?" Joe asked.

"They never found him, or the money," replied Frank. "At least at the time these stories were printed."

Joe rubbed the back of his neck. "I think we're on to something. Let's say the money was never recovered. Maybe Patch was the other robber, and he has it stashed somewhere."

"No," Frank said, shaking his head. He folded the clippings and put them back in their bags. "I don't buy it. Why would a man with two million dollars be living like this? After ten years?"

"It would explain why a policeman was hunting him," Joe suggested. "Maybe he's been hunting Patch all this time and finally found him."

"Or maybe *the cop* knows where the money is and Patch has been hunting *him* all this time," Frank said. "It makes sense—almost. Patch wanders from place to place looking for the two million some cop made off with. But why would a corrupt cop, on the run, be in uniform?"

Joe raised an eyebrow. "You're right. It almost makes sense, but not quite. Maybe the library has information on the heist. We'd better pack up this stuff and get out of here."

Frank stuffed the resealed bags into the shoes. "Of course, the clippings may not have anything to do with anything." But instinct told him they did.

Another set of headlights lit up the boat house. This time they stopped and shed a continuous glow inside the little building. A car motor was turned off, but the lights stayed on. One car door slammed.

"Someone's out there," Joe whispered. "And coming this way. The tide's too high, so we can't go out through the shack."

"Try the back window," Frank said to Joe. "We'll have to hope no one sees us go that way."

Joe was starting for the rear window of the boat house, when Frank called in a loud whisper, "Get down!" The silhouette of a man appeared at the window. The Hardys clung to the shadows and didn't move. Then the man turned away. A few seconds later the car motor started up again, and the lights backed away. It was dark again.

As soon as the car was gone, Joe was on his feet.

"Good idea," Frank said. They unbolted the window and forced it open. Frank motioned for Joe to climb through. Then Frank followed. The brothers landed on the beach beside the boat house.

But before they could run off, half a dozen shots rang out. First Joe, then Frank cried out and fell violently backward onto the sand. They lay still in the foaming surf.

Chapter

7

As THE SWITCHBLADE plunged at her throat, Callie bent down and twisted out of the way. The knife struck the wall behind her. Thrown off balance, Patch cried out in surprise and stumbled. Callie drew her head up and butted the arm still pinning her to the wall. She slipped out of Patch's reach and ran off, but stopped a few feet later when Patch didn't follow.

"Won't do you any good to run, Callie. Old Patch knows where to find you." He laughed.

"Then you *did* turn on the gas at the bottling plant," she gasped. "Why? Why do you want to kill me?"

"That man on the beach," Patch said, leaning against the wall but keeping his good eye on

Callie. "No one can connect me to him but you. No way I can let you go."

"It won't work," Callie said. "I got it all on videotape."

Patch reached into a pocket and drew out a small black case. "This one?"

"H-how?" Callie stammered. "You weren't there."

Patch raised one corner of his mouth. "Easy to pay people to do things." He dropped the video-cassette back into his pocket. Then, unexpectedly, he raised the knife again, waving it at Callie. She jumped back. "Killing, though, I do myself."

Callie hesitated for just a second, deciding whether to fight or run. She did neither. Instead, she screamed at the top of her lungs.

Patch, unfazed, shook his head and took one step closer. "No one around. No one's coming to help you now," he said menacingly.

She ran.

But then he was in front of her, grabbing at her, swinging the knife. Callie surprised him, stopped dead, and launched herself straight at him. They fell to the ground in a tangled heap. Callie got up first and started to run, but Patch's hand snaked out and caught her ankle, sending Callie stumbling forward. She landed against a garbage can set out for the morning pickup.

Callie rolled onto her back just in time to see the switchblade flashing down at her again. There was no time to think. She scuttled away crablike on her hands and feet. Her hand touched the cold metal top of the garbage can and launched it straight up at the knife.

The switchblade fell from Patch's fist and skittered along the sidewalk. Callie kicked out, driving her shoe into Patch's shin.

With a yelp of pain he hopped back and clutched at his leg. A cold rage suffused his face as Callie got back to her feet, holding the lid in front of her like a shield. "No one around, Callie," he repeated. "Can't get away from me." He stared at her, and she felt a shiver of fear ripple through her.

Her eyes fell on the switchblade lying on the pavement, and for a second she considered making a run for it. But Patch was closer to the knife. The instant she made her move he'd go for it, and she knew he'd get there first. The end of the mall seemed a million miles away.

"Come on," Patch said, beckoning her to him. "Let's finish it."

"No!" Callie screamed. She spun around and hurled the metal lid at the nearest store window like a Frisbee. A security grate kept the window from breaking, but huge cracks appeared up and down the length of it, and from inside the store came the shrill ringing of a burglar alarm.

Callie turned and ran, but her legs grew heavier with each step. The end of the mall appeared as in a dream—so close but unreachable. Her lungs were burning and she couldn't think of anything but reaching the end of the mall.

Just then rough hands reached out and grabbed her shoulders, yanking her backward. Callie felt Patch's hot, stale breath on the side of her face and heard his crude laughter in her ear. She tried to dig her fingers into his arms as he shifted and wrapped his arm around her throat. But her strength was gone. As he slowly squeezed the air from her, she thought she heard the long, loud screeching of birds.

No, a police siren, she realized. The alarm had attracted help. The police are coming.

The thought energized her, and she felt Patch hesitate and loosen his grip on her throat. She shot her arm straight out and brought it back in again, cannonballing her elbow straight into Patch's ribs and knocking the wind out of him. He let her go. Seeing him stagger, she turned and quickly pulled the videotape from his pocket, then jumped back out of his reach. As the sirens grew louder, he bolted, stopping only long enough to pick up the switchblade. Exhausted, Callie stumbled back against a building and waited for the police to arrive.

No, the police mustn't catch me either, she thought. One cop already wanted to get his hands on her, and she knew she wasn't willing to tell anyone about Patch until she got to the bottom of the mystery. Quickly, she slipped into the shadows and headed back to the beach before the police arrived.

Car lights switched on, flooding the ground around the old boat house. Frank Hardy lay facedown in the sand, his eyes closed, his arms spread to either side. A few feet away Joe Hardy sprawled just under the open window, a trickle of blood rolling down his temple. Neither of them moved.

Frank opened his eyes a slit and watched as a tall, mustached man stepped in front of the headlights. He was dressed in a police patrolman's uniform. Despite the midnight darkness, he wore wire-framed aviator sunglasses, and in his hand was a nine-millimeter automatic. As he walked toward the Hardys, he drew the clip from the pistol and slipped in a new one.

The man stood over the Hardys and studied them. Then he crouched down and nudged Joe with the barrel of the gun. No response. The man kicked him, and when again there was no response, he snickered and turned his attention to Frank.

"Wake up," the man said gruffly, and nudged Frank in the shoulder with his toe. Satisfied that Frank was out, he wedged his foot between Frank and the sand, and rolled him over for a good look at him.

As he rolled, Frank grabbed a handful of sand and flung it up into the policeman's face.

With a howl the cop staggered back and rubbed his eyes while trying to take aim at Frank.

The first shot spat sand into Frank's hair, and Frank swung his legs around, catching the cop around the ankles and pitching him to the ground.

At once Frank was on him, grappling for the gun. The policeman writhed, but Frank pinned him with his arms and legs, and crept his hand up the man's arm to his gun. As they struggled, another shot spat out, smashing into the boat house.

"Who are you?" Frank asked, peering down at the policeman's face.

For an answer the policeman slammed his knee up into Frank's back, and Frank pitched forward. Pain rushed through him as the policeman landed a haymaker in his stomach, but Frank kept his hand on the gun.

Like gladiators joined at the wrist, they rose together, each keeping a grip on the pistol. The policeman slammed an awkward left into Frank's jaw. Frank staggered back toward the surf, his hold on the pistol beginning to weaken.

Then he collected himself and tightened his hand around the man's trigger finger.

Six rapid-fire shots ripped through the sky.

Enraged, the policeman pulled back, finally breaking Frank's grip. The gun smashed down against Frank's head, and Frank tumbled back, landing at the surf's edge. He was dazed, and his arms no longer worked. A fog appeared to be swallowing him, and through that fog Frank saw the policeman aiming the pistol at his head.

Too exhausted to move, Frank merely covered his face with his hands. The policeman's finger slowly squeezed the trigger.

Click!

Frank's eyes opened wide in relief. The gun was empty.

As water washed onto Frank's hair, the policeman dropped to his knees, his hand pressed against Frank's face. The surf filled Frank's nose and mouth and forced its way down his throat. He sputtered and tried to rise, but the policeman was forcing him down.

Stay calm, he thought. Don't panic. He slowly exhaled the air still in his lungs to keep the water out, and concentrated, as he had learned to do in karate class. With great effort Frank focused on the policeman.

The heel of Frank's hand snapped up, clipping the policeman in the solar plexus. The man grunted and let go, and Frank grabbed him by the collar. He rolled back, lifting the policeman with him, and the policeman flew over his head and into the water.

Frank dragged himself onto dry land. Already the cop was staggering out of the ocean. When he saw Frank he aimed at him again and pulled the trigger twice. Again there was only a clicking. Frustrated, the policeman flung the gun at Frank, but Frank knocked it aside and dove at the man. The officer sidestepped and let Frank fall into the surf. Then the policeman ran to his car, got in, and sped off.

Frank returned to the boat house and sank to his knees next to Joe. "It's okay. It's all over." Weakly, he shook his brother, but Joe didn't move.

Then Frank noticed the blood on Joe's head, and a horrifying thought sprang into his mind.

Joe wasn't unconscious. He was dead.

Chapter

8

"FRANK?" JOE RASPED weakly. "What happened?"

He tried to sit up, but his eyes screwed shut in pain and he flopped down again, hand to his bleeding head.

"Joe!" Frank shouted, ecstatic. "You're alive! Lie still while I go get help. You've been shot."

Joe propped himself up on one arm. The pain in his head was receding into a dull throb. "Was I?" he said. "Oh, I remember now. Someone was shooting at us."

"The policeman," said Frank. "I chased him off, but I couldn't catch him."

"When I heard the shots, I dove for cover, same as you," Joe continued. Slowly, he raised himself to a sitting position, and this time he didn't collapse. "But I was diving *away* from the shots. There's no way a bullet could have grazed my head. My leg or arm, maybe, but not my head."

"But your head's bleeding," Frank said.

Joe began to crawl, patting the sand all around him. "Maybe I hit it when I was falling. Something sharp, metal . . ." His hand slapped down near the wall of the boat house, and he let out a sharp cry. "I think I found something."

"Buried treasure on the beach," Frank said. "Give me a break." But he quickly began to brush sand away from the spot Joe indicated. An object became visible near the wall of the building. "You're right, there is something here. Looks like a file box of some sort."

"Patch's?"

"Maybe. It'd explain what the shovel in the shack was for."

Joe had almost forgotten the ache in his head as he lifted up the small green-painted metal box that was carefully sealed in a plastic bag.

"It sure wasn't deep," Joe said. "Patch isn't much at burying things."

"*If* it's his," Frank warned. "We don't know that yet. Anyway, he might have been in a hurry." He ran his fingers over the bag around the box. "I don't think this has been here long. How's your head?" he asked Joe as he peeled off the plastic.

"I'll live," said Joe. "What's in the box?" Frank popped open the lid. He lifted up the contents of the box to inspect them by the light of the passing cars.

"Photographs," Frank said, bewildered. "Just old photos." They were brown with age.

Joe picked one from the box and studied it intently as another car passed on the road. "The developing date was over ten years ago. Just like Patch's newspaper clippings."

In the photo in his hand were two men, one tall and handsome, with long, wavy hair, and the other slightly shorter and blond, with a broad smile. They were in swim trunks, at a beach, and were posing with their hands on each other's shoulders.

"Moran," Frank said, looking over Joe's shoulder.

"What?"

"The blond guy. His picture was in the paper. That's Sam Moran, the thief who got killed. But who's his buddy?"

"You think maybe . . ." Joe began.

Frank shrugged. "The other guy could be Moran's partner. Maybe." He plucked the photo from Joe's hand, folded it down the middle, and bent it back so that only the unknown man was looking up at him, and stuffed the picture in his pocket. "I'll lay odds it's Patch. Maybe Callie can identify him for us."

Joe picked up another picture of the unknown man and closed the box. "It'll be dawn soon," he said. "We'd better get out of here before Patch decides to show up. Neither of us looks like we could bear up under another fight."

They looked at themselves in their torn, wet clothes. Frank grinned, and a single chuckle burst from his lips. Then Joe began to crack up, and Frank joined the laughter.

"Yeah, it's been a long night," Frank said when they stopped. "Otherwise none of this would seem even slightly funny. Come on, let's pack up here and go get some sleep."

They wrapped up the box and reburied it.

Callie stood alone in the shadow of the bottling plant. Far in the east were the first traces of morning, a faint lightening of the gray sky.

Callie paced, wondering what had become of Frank and Joe. Every sound made her jump, and now the videotape in her bag seemed too heavy for her to carry. She wanted to throw it into the ocean.

I'm just tired, she thought, and sat on a crate next to the factory to rest and close her eyes for a minute. Before she knew it, she was asleep.

She woke to distant voices. The sky was lighter—soon the sun would break the horizon. How long have I been asleep, she wondered. A rush of panic swept through her. She dug frantically through her bags for the videotape. It was still there.

The voices were gone. But now heavy footsteps echoed on the concrete sidewalk around the corner of the building, heading straight for her. She looked around for a place to hide, but there was nothing but beach, and once on the beach they would see her. Frantically, she stood and stamped her foot down on the crate, breaking it.

She picked up a flat board from the crate, crept to the corner of the building, and waited. The footsteps had stopped at the sound of the breaking crate, but then they started again. Callie sensed a presence just around the corner, not six inches away. She could feel her heart pounding. She gritted her teeth and tightened her grip on the board.

As a head came into view, she slammed the board down. But the figure had twisted aside at the last minute and stomped on the wood as it hit the ground. The board snapped into bits. Callie screamed and backed away, cuffing her arms over her face.

"Callie?" said Frank. "What are you doing? What's wrong?"

She hurled herself into his arms and buried her face in his chest. "Oh, Frank. I'm so glad you're back. It's been just an awful night."

"We know," said Joe, joining them. "It's been bad for us too. What happened to you?"

She pulled away from Frank and straightened up, trying to regain her composure. "Nothing I couldn't handle," she said defensively. "I thought something had happened to *you*."

"We're more or less okay," said Frank. "The big question now is: where are we going to sleep?" He looked at Joe's dirty face and torn shirt and Callie's grubby outfit, and wondered what he himself looked like. "We can't go back to your aunt's house. The policeman knows about her." He stared at the bottling plant. "I don't much like the idea of staying here but no hotel's going to let us in looking like this."

"Oh, I don't know," Callie said. She rooted through her pockets and finally came out with a credit card. "We could try. Credit talks, right? Don't leave home without it."

Frank stretched as he put on his shirt. Four hours of sleep in the once stylish but now seedy motel had refreshed him. He felt ready to follow Patch's trail. Catching Patch and the policeman was, he decided, the only way to make sure Callie would be safe.

"I'm going next door to check on Callie," he said to Joe as Joe stepped out of the shower. Still half asleep, his brother yawned and nodded, obviously too sleepy to care. Frank stepped out of the motel room and shut the door behind him.

Despite their problems, he was, he realized, in a good mood.

His mood shifted abruptly as he rapped on Callie's door. It creaked open.

No one was inside the room. The bedcovers were thrown to one side, and in a pile on the floor were Callie's clothes and the bags she had been carrying. Frank pounded on the wall adjoining their rooms.

"Joe! Get over here now!"

When Joe, shoeless and shirtless, dashed into the room, he found Frank going through the bags. "What was all the pounding about? What's up?"

Frank turned. His face was grave. "They took Callie, Joe. She's gone!"

Chapter

9

"WHAT'S GOING ON here?" said an angry voice behind the Hardys.

"Oh," said Joe, grinning at Frank's shock and embarrassment. "Hi, Callie."

Frank glanced at his brother, then turned to face Callie. She was now dressed in khaki slacks, tan sandals, and a T-shirt with *California* written on the front. In her hand was a shopping bag. Sunglasses covered her eyes, and a large purse was slung over her shoulder.

"Uh—you're not kidnapped," Frank said.

"Of course not," Callie replied, puzzled. "There's a great store in the lobby, and—" She pointed at the rags at Frank's feet. "I couldn't wander around in those all day. You'd better change clothes too."

"We'd like to," said Joe, "but the butler hasn't laid out our clean ones yet."

"That's why I picked up a little something for each of you." She reached into the shopping bag, took out a green knit shirt and chinos, and tossed them to Frank. "You'll look good in those."

Then she pulled out a short-sleeved Hawaiian shirt in a red, yellow, and orange flower print and handed it to Joe.

He unfolded it and pulled it over his head. "I'm supposed to wear this?" he asked in dismay. "I look like a tourist!"

"It's you, Joe," Callie said. "This is surfer town, remember? You'll blend right in."

"Enough, you two," said Frank, slipping into his new shirt. "I'm not finished with Callie." He turned to her angrily. "You had no right to go off without telling us—" he began.

"I'm sorry. I really should have told you where I was going, Frank," she said.

"It's okay," Frank replied. They reached for each other's hands.

"Let's get out of here and do something," Joe said.

"Yeah, let's stop by the campus," Callie said. "There's something there I want to look at."

They left the motel and walked to the corner to wait for a bus. Joe looked around, watching for the smallest sign they were being followed, while Frank dug into his pocket.

"Recognize this man?" Frank asked Callie. He showed her the photograph from Patch's file box. It was the tall man with the long hair.

Callie shook her head. "Should I?"

Frank sighed with disappointment. "I thought he might be your friend Patch."

"Patch is not my friend, and he doesn't look at all like that," Callie said. "Why?"

The bus appeared, and they climbed on, taking the seats next to the back door. Frank caught Callie up on what they had discovered on the beach. Joe didn't like giving Callie any more information than they had to, but he knew there wasn't much he could do about it. Like it or not, Callie was involved.

Quickly, Callie gave the Hardys the story of her meeting with Patch at the mall—toning down the violence considerably though. "And look what he had with him—this," she concluded, dramatically pulling the black videotape from her bag.

Frank's and Joe's eyes widened in surprise. "Why didn't you tell us you'd gotten it back?" Frank said angrily. "You've been holding out, Callie."

"No, I haven't. This isn't even the right tape. I stashed the one with Patch and the policeman at the UCLA tape lab yesterday, after I talked to you."

"Then why were you upset when this was stolen?"

Callie smiled. "This tape was worthless to Patch, but it was vital to me. I'd switched the real tape for this one at the lab. The only way I can get the right tape is to bring this one back and switch again, before the tape librarian notices that this one's missing and contacts the last person who checked it out—me."

Joe frowned. "Pretty complicated."

"Yeah, but so's this case," Frank said. "Let's see what we've got so far. Okay?" Callie and Joe nodded.

"Okay, we've got a policeman handing a briefcase to a bum, then trying to kill him. What does that suggest?"

"Patch was, or is, blackmailing the policeman," Joe said. "The cop wants him out of the way."

"Right. And both of them want anyone who can put them together, like Callie, gone. So neither of them wants to risk exposure. Patch has a collection of newspaper articles about a robbery, and has a collection of photos of a dead man known to have been involved in the robbery."

"So Patch and the robbery must somehow be connected," Callie concluded. The bus lurched to a stop across from the gate to UCLA. "Here's our stop."

They piled off the bus and crossed the street, heading onto campus.

"Let's head for the video lab," Frank said. "I want to have a look at that tape."

"All right, but I've looked," Callie replied. "I've looked and looked, and there's nothing on it that gives us any more information."

"You're missing something," Frank insisted. "You must be."

Within minutes they reached the video lab. But as they pushed through the door, Callie's face dropped. Every seat in the room was taken. "It's full," she said. "We'll have to come back later."

Frank nodded. "Okay. In the meantime, I'd like to take another look at those newspaper clippings. I couldn't see them too well last night."

"But we left them back at the beach," Joe said. "So Patch wouldn't notice them missing."

Frank turned to Callie. "They were from a Philadelphia newspaper, September or so, ten years ago. Is there a library around here?"

"This is UCLA," Callie replied. "It has one of the best libraries in the country." They left the video lab and strolled back out onto the private street that ran the length of the campus.

"Good," Frank said. "I'd like all the background we can get."

They had to wait half an hour before a projector became available, and Frank, Joe, and Callie crowded into a cramped booth to watch the tiny screen. Callie brought two rolls of microfilm, each with a month's worth of newspapers photographed on them. She slipped them into the projector.

Joe rolled the film to the date Frank had read on Patch's clippings. "Here it is," he said. "Headline stuff. Pretty much what you said, two guys knock over an armored car and take off."

"Anything about who they were?"

"Not yet." He rolled the film ahead to the next day. "Here's a little more. Details about how the cops spotted them as they took off through some drainage grates. No mention of names yet though."

When he reached the newspaper for the third day after the robbery, Joe said, "Bingo. Seems the guard on the armored car picked Sam Moran out of the mug books."

"But he died before they could catch him," Frank said. "And they never identified his partner?"

Joe scanned through the next week's stories. "Nope. No partner, no money. We've got nothing more than before." Suddenly he froze, and adjusted the focus on the projector. "Here's something. Wait."

"What is it?" said Callie.

"Uh-huh, uh-huh," Joe mumbled, reading the story. "You know they found Moran and he was burned to a crisp . . . well, at least his face was."

Frank nodded.

"Seems they found enough I.D. to identify him," Joe said. "Maybe dental records. And he had some money on him that was burned too. But it was definitely identified as part of the heist. The cops figured he was rigging some sort of bomb and it went off in his face."

Frank sat back and rubbed his neck. "Interesting. Our Mr. Moran was an expert in explosives. Odd sideline for a heist man."

"Read his specialty," Joe said.

"Well, well," Frank replied, peering at the screen. "Molotov cocktails. Like the one that almost fried Emma's house."

"What?" cried Callie, outraged. "You never told me about that. What else have you been keeping from me?"

The Hardys looked at her in sheepish silence. "Nothing," Frank said. "Have you called her yet?"

"Yeah, this morning, I let her know I was all right," Callie answered. "Let me see this." She gently pushed Frank's shoulders down so she could stare at the screen.

Callie screamed and clapped her hand over her mouth to muffle the sound. "That man," she said, pointing at the screen. "That man."

Frank and Joe looked at the photograph that went with the story. "Don't worry about him,"

Frank assured her. "That's Sam Moran. He's the one who died."

"That's not Sam Moran," Callie gasped. "At least, not anymore. And he's not dead."

She stared at the picture.

"His name is Patch."

Chapter
10

"YOU'RE SURE?" FRANK asked. "The picture's ten years old. Look at it again and take your time."

"I don't have to look," she answered. "I saw him last night. That's him. Don't you see? Moran kills someone and burns the body. Then he fixes the dental records somehow and leaves the poor guy to be taken for him. That's what he meant when he said he'd killed before."

"It doesn't fit," said Frank. "Patch doesn't have any money or he wouldn't be living the way he does. So where'd the two million dollars go?" He leaned his head back and gaped at Callie. "What did you mean a minute ago? Did he try to kill you?"

Callie nodded guiltily.

"You should have told me!"

"You didn't tell me about someone firebombing Aunt Emma's house. It's the same thing."

"It's not," Frank insisted.

"Stop it!" Joe said. "From now on, everyone tells everyone everything, okay?" He checked his watch. "I think we've got all we can get here. How about trying the video room again?"

"All right," Callie said, and stormed out of the booth. Frank stomped silently after her, his shoulders hunched and hands rammed into his pockets. Slipping the microfilm off the projector, Joe shrugged his shoulders and muttered to himself, "Young love."

Much larger than the cramped microfiche cubicles in the library, the video booth was carpeted and soundproofed, with a large television and a videocassette player attached to a moving cart. In a semicircle around the cart were a few padded gray chairs. Frank was sitting in one and tapping his foot impatiently.

"Where is she?" he asked, looking over his shoulder and through the opening into the video lab. He found Callie standing at a large desk, speaking to a middle-aged woman in glasses.

"Oh, she's all right," said Joe. Stretching his legs, he slouched in the chair next to Frank.

"Here she comes."

Callie entered, carrying a videocassette, and

slammed the door behind her. "They didn't want me to check it out, do you believe it? A school videotape. I wonder if they suspected anything." She opened the black case in her hand, took out the cassette, and slipped it into the videoplayer. Glancing furtively around to make sure no one outside the room was watching her, she drew the other cassette from her purse and slipped it into the case.

"Well, they've got their precious tape back," she said, picking up a remote control and plopping down in the chair next to Joe's. Her thumb jammed the button marked play. "This set's equipped with a special-effects generator, so if you want to do anything fancy, let me know." There was an edge in her voice that made Joe uneasy.

The tape began rolling. "So that's Patch, huh?" Frank said as a shabby man crept onto the screen. All around was empty beach. Patch's head popped up suddenly, as if someone had called his name.

"Callie's right," said Joe. "That's Moran. Wonder what happened to his eye?"

The policeman stepped into view, wearing his dark aviator sunglasses. In his hand was a pigskin briefcase edged in chrome. Patch poked greedy fingers at it.

"I wish you had gotten sound," Frank said.

"Sorry it wasn't a good enough job for the

great detective," Callie replied coolly. "The noise of the surf blotted out everything."

"Can we get close-ups out of this thing?" Joe suggested. "If we can, maybe we can read their lips."

Frank shook his head. "They're moving around too much. We'd get only a bit of it at most, and then there's no way of knowing if we're right. Not worth the effort.

"Hold it!" Frank ordered, and Callie hit the freeze-frame button. Patch had opened the briefcase, and the policeman had drawn his gun, and now the policeman faced the camera, frozen in midmovement.

Frank slapped his forehead. "I should have realized this on the beach. I knew when we were fighting that something about that guy didn't jibe."

Joe and Callie stared at him. "What do you mean?" Joe asked.

"Look." Frank walked to the television and ran his finger across the bottom of the screen. "He's wearing sneakers with a regulation police uniform. Whoever he is, he's not on duty. Maybe he's not a cop at all."

"Then where did he get the uniform?" asked Callie. "Costume shops don't rent police uniforms—it's against the law. And to get one from a uniform store you have to prove you're a cop." She paused. "He could be a cop with bad feet."

Frank sank back in his chair and scowled.

"Don't sulk," Callie scolded.

"Bring his face in tight, Callie," Joe said. She pressed another button, and the policeman's face filled the screen. "Good. Frank, give me that picture you lifted from Patch." Frank dug the photo out and handed it to Joe, who patted his own pocket. "Anyone got a pen or pencil?"

Callie handed him a pen, and for a few seconds Joe scrawled on the photograph. He handed the pen back to Callie and pressed the photo against the screen.

"Back it up so the heads on the screen and in the picture are the same size, and come up here," he demanded.

Puzzled, Frank and Callie stepped up for a look. The photograph, now with a mustache and a pair of sunglasses drawn on the mystery man's face, was identical to the video image of the policeman, except for the long wavy hair. Frank groaned in disbelief.

"It was in front of us all the time," he said. "How could we have missed it?"

"You mean—?" Callie began.

"Right," Joe replied. "The cop is really the other thief. That puts our blackmail theory back in business."

Excited, Frank paced back and forth, thinking

out loud. "Of course. Now it's starting to make sense. Moran—Patch—gets rooked out of his share of the money. He runs into his old partner out here and tries to force him to hand over the money."

"It's sketchy," Joe said. "But it's a start."

"And I've seen both of them," Callie said with a shudder. "That explains why neither wants me alive. Both could go to jail."

The Hardys stood outside the video room as Callie returned the black case, with the original videocassette inside, to the desk. As they reached the door of the video lab, an Oriental woman in her late thirties entered and smiled at them. "Hello, Callie."

Smiling back, Callie stopped and said, "Hi, Ms. Ki." She gestured to the Hardys. "These are friends of mine from out of town, Frank and Joe." To them she said, "This is Ms. Ki. She's in charge of my program."

Ms. Ki held out her hand, and in turn the Hardys shook it. "My pleasure," she said. "Callie, what did you do at Meteoric yesterday morning? The studio called up after the field trip to ask about you—where you lived and all. The man said they were thinking of offering you a screen test!"

"Screen test?"

"Have you heard from them yet? I told them

you're interested in journalism, not acting, but they wouldn't listen to me."

"No," Callie said, still dazed. "But I haven't been home much. I'll check with my aunt—"

"Well." Ms. Ki gave them another big smile. "Break a leg."

"Thank you," Callie said. Ms. Ki went into the video lab, and Callie and the Hardys left the building.

"Meteoric Studios?" Frank asked when they were outside.

"We took a tour there yesterday. I had just been to the video lab and remembered the production class field trip . . ." Callie said, trailing off. All of a sudden her eyes widened. "It was later yesterday afternoon, after I witnessed Patch's meeting with the policeman and after the field trip, that the policeman showed up at school asking about me. And that was the last I thought about the field trip. Is it important?"

Frank snapped his fingers, an intense look on his face. *"Now* I know what else about that cop was bothering me."

"What?" Joe asked, excited.

"His badge. It didn't have a number on it. We could go back and check on the videotape, but I'm sure—"

"No need to do that," Joe said. "Now that you mention it, I remember too." He groaned. "How could we have missed that for so long?"

"So what?" asked Callie. "I don't get it."

"So the uniform *must* be a costume," Joe explained to her. "A real policeman would have removed his badge altogether if he didn't want to be identified. Better yet, he wouldn't wear a uniform at all."

"But with a fake badge and no regulation shoes, chances are very good it's a costume," Frank continued. "And if what you say about it being illegal to rent a police uniform is true—"

"Then he must have swiped it from a—a studio wardrobe—" said Callie.

"Bingo!" said Frank. He and Joe beamed at her.

Callie beamed back. "So, this bank robber works at Meteoric Studios and saw me there yesterday, after he saw me on the beach."

"It's a long shot," Frank answered. "But it's the only solution that makes any sense. The 'studio' did call your professor to find out about you."

As they turned the corner of the building, their thoughts were broken by an engine revving to life. A car on a blocked-off street? Callie wondered for a second. Suddenly a van squealed into motion, racing right toward them.

"This way," Joe shouted, ducking into an alley. As the van zoomed closer, Frank grabbed Callie and pulled her into the alley too. "Don't!" yelled Joe. "It's a dead end. Get out!"

As if the driver had heard them, the van wheeled around and careened into the alley.

Joe reached the dead end and pressed in vain against the wall. "No good," he yelled. "Solid brick."

His words were drowned out by the roar of the engine as the huge van bore down on them.

Chapter
11

"FRANK," CALLIE SCREAMED. "What are we going to do?"

Frank barely heard her. "We'll flatten ourselves against the side wall, you go under," he yelled to Joe, keeping his eyes on the onrushing van. In the middle of the narrow alley, flush against the back wall, Joe began to tense.

"Now!" Joe yelled. Frank slammed an arm across Callie, flattening himself on top of her against the wall. Joe fell to the ground, directly in the path of the van. He pulled his arms in tight to his body to avoid the spinning tires and rolled safely under the center of the van.

The van just brushed against Frank and Callie and smashed into the back wall. From inside the van came the wail of a car horn. It didn't stop.

"Joe!" Frank called. Although the van had missed them, the crackup had them pinned in the corner. "Are you all right?"

"Fine," came Joe's voice from under the van. "Get the driver."

"We can't," Callie shouted. "No room to open the door." The driver ducked his head and covered his face with his hand. His head down, he stumbled through the van and out the back door.

"Got him," Joe said. His hand snaked out from under the van's rear bumper and caught the driver's ankle as he hit the ground. But the driver didn't trip. His other heel ground down on Joe's wrist, and Joe splayed his fingers in pain, releasing the man's leg.

In a flash the driver sprinted to the end of the alley and vanished.

Joe crawled out from under the van, wincing and massaging the pain from his hand. "Hold on," he told Frank and Callie as he climbed in the back of the van. Then he was in the driver's seat and closed the driver's door.

"Can you get us out?" Frank asked.

Joe looked at the dashboard. There were no keys in the ignition, but two colored wires dangled from the steering column. "Just a minute. I think it was hot-wired."

"Stolen?" Callie said.

"Probably," Joe said. "Most people don't use their own cars to run other people down." He leaned over, grabbed the two wires, and touched the exposed ends together. The van rumbled to life. Joe shifted to reverse.

With a tortured whine of metal scraping cement, Joe backed the van out of the alley, leaving trails of silver paint along the alley wall. Frank and Callie followed him out, and were waiting for him when Joe climbed out of the van.

"Who was driving?" Joe asked. "Patch or the policeman?"

"We didn't get a chance to look," Frank replied. "Our next job is going to be finding out who this so-called policeman is."

"How do we do that?" Callie said. "Head for Meteoric Studios?"

"No," Frank said sternly. "Joe and I go. You go into hiding, somewhere safe." Callie got ready to argue.

Joe stepped in. "Frank, you know under most circumstances I'd agree with you. But you know Callie's not going to leave the city. It's her case, her story. We'd never let anyone cut us out of a case, and you know Callie's no different. Anyway, there's nowhere for her to go. She wasn't safe with the street people, and she won't be safe with her aunt. At least with us she'll be protected."

For a long moment Frank stared at Joe. "Okay," he said finally. Callie smiled.

"Thanks, Joe," she said.

"Don't mention it," Joe replied. "And I mean that. Don't *ever* mention it again."

In a valley between two mountains in the Hollywood Hills lay Meteor Town. In the 1970s it had almost closed, saved at the last minute by the surprise success of one of its low-budget movies. Since then Meteoric Studios had grown to be one of the largest film production companies in the world, so large that now it brought in thousands of tourists daily.

Frank stood at the ticket booth at the main gate. "Three adult tickets, please," he said politely. When money and tickets had changed hands, he joined Joe and Callie at the entrance.

"We're in," said Joe. "Any ideas on where we start looking for this policeman?"

"I think we should join a tour group," Frank said. "They'll take us everywhere, and that way we won't attract any attention. Just three more tourists sight-seeing." Callie had her sunglasses propped on her head. Frank gently lowered them over her eyes, saying, "Keep yourself disguised as much as possible. Remember, the cop knows what you look like. We don't want to tip him off."

Callie removed the sunglasses and put them in her purse. "He knows your faces too. Who'll blow whose cover? Anyway, what are the odds we'll run into him?"

"That's just it," Joe reminded her. "We won't know until it's too late. We don't really know what he looks like now, without his sunglasses and mustache, only what he looked like ten years ago."

Silently, the three of them got in line behind a group of people being corralled into small railway cars. The small railway, Frank could see, looped all through Meteor Town. In keeping with the studio's outer-space image, the cars were designed as rocket ships, with a dozen or so people to a car. Frank, Callie, and Joe got into the first car and sat down. Metal bars folded down over their laps to keep them in their seats.

"You may get out at each rocket stop," said the tour guide, a slender, dark-haired woman in a shiny silver suit who stood at the front of the rocket. "But while the rocket is in motion, it's very important you stay seated for your own safety."

She cleared her throat. "Welcome to the Meteoric Studios tour. For the next two hours you'll be learning all about the wonderful world of movies, and how the things you see on the big screen are done. There will be a refreshment stop halfway through, and if we're lucky, we may see some actual filming. If you have any questions, be sure to ask. Now, if everyone's ready, let's blast off."

She sounds like she's reading a script, Joe

thought. A loud roar came over the loudspeakers, then a hiss like a rush of air, and the car lurched forward, throwing everyone back in their seats. After a second the pressure died, and the car wobbled slowly along the tracks.

To his left Joe saw a small arena, where other tourists were gathered to watch stunt cars crashing.

The rocket train chugged along the edge of the Meteor Town parking lot, then turned sharply to the left. Suddenly the car sped up, rushing headlong toward solid rock ahead. Surprised passengers began to scream and tug at the braces holding them in their seats, but the braces held firm.

The rock parted into strips of cloth that spread harmlessly around the car, and the train passed through a man-made tunnel.

"You've been tricked by illusions," the tour guide revealed. "We never sped up. Images were projected onto a screen"—she gestured at the strips of cloth now hanging straight down again to look like a solid wall—"and we increased the speed at which those images changed."

"In other words," Frank piped up, "because it looked like we were going faster, we thought it felt like we were going faster."

"Right," said the tour guide, looking at him approvingly. Frank smiled back at her, and Callie gave him a slight nudge with her elbow.

They left the tunnel and stopped in front of a

concrete building, with large sliding doors, that looked like an airplane hangar. The train's seat braces slid aside. "Everyone follow me," the tour guide said. The group filed into the building and stood in front of a stage.

A blond young man in a jumpsuit, with a smile as bright as the tour guide's, stepped onto the stage. He wore a holster with a six-shooter in it. "Hi," he said loudly, and all the tourists shouted, "Hi!" back. "I'm Peter," he continued. "Ever wonder how we do those shootouts on television?" A resounding yes roared from the group, and the young man named Peter rambled on.

As Peter spoke, a rope dropped from the ceiling behind him, and a ninja, garbed head to toe in black, slithered down it to the floor. The audience made warning noises, but Peter seemed not to notice. Drawing a sword from a scabbard strapped to his leg, the ninja raised it to plunge into Peter's back.

Suddenly Peter drew his six-gun and spun. Two shots went off, and the ninja fell backward, blood spreading across his chest. The hall filled with screams.

The ninja leapt to his feet, and he and the young man bowed to the crowd. "That was done with something we call a squib," said Peter. He set the six-shooter down behind him and drew a small wad out of his pocket as the ninja left the stage. "It's a little packet of jelly with a tiny explosive charge that we sew into clothing. When a gunshot using blanks is fired, these little packs of jelly are exploded with a radio signal. It makes it look like someone has been shot. Come on, I want two volunteers to try it.''

No one moved, but the tour guide stepped behind Frank and Joe and cocked her head toward them. "How about you?" Peter asked Frank and Joe, and amid a hail of applause the Hardys took the stage.

Peter slipped a quilted jacket onto Joe. "This young man wears a jacket filled with squibs," he told the audience. He stepped to Frank and handed him the gun. "Now this young man is going to kill him, just as he would on TV."

As Peter cried, "Ready!" Frank aimed the gun. "Aim!"

Joe grinned broadly and swaggered a little, hamming it up for the audience. Then he looked back at Frank and his grin froze. He blinked in astonishment. Frank didn't have the prop six-gun in his hands, but a .44 revolver. The gun aimed at his chest was real.

"Frank—" he cried, reaching out toward his brother.

"Fire!" commanded Peter.

Frank's finger squeezed the trigger.

Chapter

12

THE GUNSHOT ROARED in Joe's ears. He felt something explode against his chest, knocking him backward. Stunned, he staggered two paces, touched his hand to his collarbone, and looked at the smear leaking across his fingers.

Red jelly. The gun was a phony after all.

"Quite a kick, eh?" said Peter cheerfully, and the audience began to laugh and clap. He slipped the squib jacket off Joe. "Even the tiny blast you get from a squib will make you totter if you're not ready for it. Our actors are trained so that they know what to expect." He shook hands first with Joe, then with Frank, and led them to the stairs and off the stage. "Let's have a big round of applause for my two partners."

"Frank, you're as white as a ghost," Callie

said as the Hardys returned to the floor. "It was just a stunt."

"Callie," Frank began, then turned to look at Joe with horrified eyes. He whispered, "You know, I almost killed you just now. That was a real gun."

"I thought so." A shiver rippled through Joe. "I "I suspected it was, but when nothing happened . . ."

"You didn't see what I saw," Frank continued. "I wasn't aiming at you. I'd never do that, not even as a joke. I shot to one side, and I saw dust fly up where the bullet hit the wall. We're just lucky a curtain kept the audience from seeing. It was real all right."

"I doubt that forty-fours are a regular part of the act," Joe concluded. "That means we've been spotted."

"This way," the tour guide said, pointing the tourists out the door. "We have lots more to see before we go back to the rockets."

Frank and Joe hung back, watching as the rest of the audience left. "Go with them, Callie," Frank said. She opened her mouth to protest, but he cut her off. "We'll catch up as soon as we can, but someone needs to stick with the tour in case we don't find anything."

"Oh, all right," Callie said with a sigh. "Be careful."

"We will," Frank replied. "Whatever you do, don't get separated from the tour."

After one last, doubtful look, Callie followed the others out. Frank and Joe started back up to the stage as Peter reappeared from the curtains.

"What are you boys doing here?" he asked uncertainly. "The tour's moved on." Peter wasn't smiling now.

"We want to talk to you about your gun," Frank said.

Suddenly Peter spun and bolted through the curtains. The Hardys ran up the stairs, pushing through the black cloth backing the stage. The backstage area was cluttered with mannequins and half-finished sets. Smears of paint had been carelessly left everywhere.

"There he goes!" said Joe as Peter ducked behind some woodwork. Sprinting, Joe began closing the gap between them. Peter reached an emergency door. It swung open, and Joe knew they'd lose him if Peter got outside.

He dove, sliding across the smooth, paint-spattered floor, and tackled Peter. They fell together to the floor. Desperately, Peter kicked Joe away. Joe scrambled to his feet and watched in awe as Peter performed a perfect backflip. In one motion he stood up and swung at Joe. Joe ducked the blow and slammed his fist into the young man's stomach, forcing the wind out of him. Peter dropped to his knees, clutching his gut.

"Now can we talk about the gun?" Joe asked as he and Frank surrounded him.

Still kneeling, Peter held up his hand. "I didn't know it was real," he said. "Not until you shot it during the act."

"You didn't seem too surprised about it," Joe said, and raised his fist menacingly.

"It's part of my job," Peter protested. "Even when things don't go right I have to make everything seem routine."

"Is killing tourists routine around here?" Joe shouted at him. "How come it happened when *we* were onstage? Why'd you choose us?"

"I didn't," Peter said. "I follow signals. The tour guides figure out who's the likeliest to go along with us, and they point out volunteers to me."

"So our tour guide set us up?"

"I don't know," Peter insisted. "She checked with Mr. Bates first, and he okayed it."

"Bates?" Frank said, puzzled. "Who's that?"

Peter stared at him. "You never heard of Stuart Bates? He's chairman of the board. He *runs* Meteoric Studios."

"Why would he bother with something like this?" Joe asked.

"He likes to come around to watch the crowds," Peter explained. "I don't know why. He never talks to me."

"You saw him okay us for the act?"

"It was funny. It looked to me like he suggested you, and your guide went along with it."

Frank took it all in. "When did Bates take over Meteoric Studios?"

"Eight or nine years ago," Peter said. "He saved the studio when it was about to go bankrupt. He financed the picture that put Meteoric back on its feet."

Joe unclenched his hand. To Frank he said, "Remember what we heard? That was almost a decade ago."

Frank nodded. "Two million dollars would go a long way toward financing a small movie. I bet the chairman of the board can get into wardrobe anytime he wants."

"So he gets us into a deadly situation and switches the gun," Joe guessed. "Makes sense."

"No," said Peter. "Mr. Bates was in the audience the whole time. He couldn't have touched the gun."

Both of them turned to Peter. Joe grabbed his collar and jerked him to his feet. "You've been lying to us. *You* were the one who rigged the gun."

"No!" Peter insisted. "I don't touch the guns. It's Jim. The ninja. He sets up all the props."

"So where—" Joe began. But he had no chance to finish.

"Joe," Frank yelled.

A black-gloved hand had shoved a stiletto through a flat that Joe was standing in front of.

Joe threw himself to the floor and rolled away just in time to see the knife slash down at him.

Frank caught the hand, slammed it twice against his leg, and the hand dropped the knife. Joe kicked it away. With a shout Frank spun and jerked the arm over his shoulder. The ninja tore through the flat and landed with a thud on his back.

He kicked up, catching Frank in the shin and knocking him off balance. Joe clipped the ninja in the arm with a right hook, and the ninja stumbled back, stopping in front of a chair. He picked it up and brought it down hard against Joe's shoulder.

Joe stood there, as surprised as the ninja was that he was unharmed. "A breakaway chair," he said amazed. "Another prop."

The ninja ducked Joe's punch, only to walk into a karate chop from Frank. He reeled back into some more flats. Frantically, he pulled on them, and they cascaded down on the Hardys. By the time Frank and Joe freed themselves, the ninja was gone.

"That solves the mystery of the switched guns," Joe said, getting to his feet. He picked up the fallen switchblade. "At least he lost his tooth-pick."

"Oh, no," said Peter. His eyes rested on a young man, who lay unconscious in his under-wear, bound and gagged behind the fallen screens. *"That's* Jim!"

"Then who was in the ninja suit?" Frank wondered out loud. Quickly, they untied the young man and slapped his cheek to wake him up. His eyes finally fluttered open.

"Who did this to you?" Joe asked.

"Never saw him before," the young man said weakly. "Never."

"You'll be okay," Frank comforted. "What did he look like?"

"Didn't see much. Only a patch over an eye."

Frank and Joe looked at each other in dismay. "Patch!" said Frank. To Peter he said, "Can you take care of your friend?"

"Sure."

"How do we get to where the tour is now?"

"They should be looking at the computerized special effects generators now," Peter said. He gave them directions, and the Hardys ran through the emergency door.

"Great," said Joe. "If we're right about Bates, we've got two killers loose on the grounds."

"And we left Callie alone." Frank's voice was tight as he led the way. "We've got to find her." They reached another building and flung open the door.

The tour was gathered around a television screen, watching pictures of people chosen from their group being projected into computer-generated backgrounds. Frank grabbed the tour guide's arm.

"Where's Callie?" he whispered.

Confused, she replied, "Who?"

"The girl I came with," he snapped impatiently. "She's supposed to be here."

The tour guide gazed across the crowd and pointed toward an open door at the far end of the hall. "She was over there just a minute ago. I have to ask you not to leave the tour again. If there's any problem—"

Before she could finish, Frank hurried out the door. It opened onto a small green lawn lined with food stands. Frank turned in circles, surveying the area, but Callie was nowhere.

"Callie," he called out. There was no answer. *"Callie!"*

"Frank," Joe said. He stopped by a wastebasket, pulled out a videocassette, and held it up for Frank to see.

Frank's heart sank. "She would never have given that up unless she—unless she—"

He couldn't bring himself to say it. Callie was gone.

Chapter

13

"HEY!" A MAN in a work suit shouted. "You can't go in there!"

Callie Shaw ignored the warning. Her lungs burned and her legs ached from running, and she needed a place to rest. From the moment she had seen Patch, dressed all in black except for his head, she had been on the move, racing from set to set in Meteor Town.

The sign on the barricade said Out of Order. No Admittance. Recklessly, Callie climbed over the gate, rolled onto the ground, and looked behind her to see if the man decided to pursue her. She was safe.

And there was no sign of Patch.

She relaxed and sat with her back to the gate. Would anyone find the tape, she wondered. Even if Patch caught her, she suspected, he wouldn't kill her until he knew where it was. If she escaped, chances were she could collect it before anyone noticed it was there. In the meantime she had time to think. Had Patch run into Frank and Joe? If so, what had he done with them?

Just then a black-gloved hand clapped onto her shoulder through the chain-link gate, and Callie screamed. "Callie," Patch whispered triumphantly. "Come out and play." His fingers dug into her skin.

She drove her fingernails into the back of Patch's hand. He snapped it away, and Callie was on her feet, running again. She didn't need to look to know Patch would quickly be over the fence and on her trail.

Think, she told herself as she ran for her life. What would Frank and Joe do?

She came to the top of a hill. Below were the tracks for the tourist trains. She scampered toward them. Eventually, the tracks would loop back to the exit, showing her the way out.

All I have to do, she told herself, is stay ahead of Patch until I get there. Easy to think, she knew from experience, but harder to do.

The tracks led into the set of a small town. To her left Callie saw a library, and to her right a town hall with a bell tower on top. The streets were lined with stores: a five-and-dime, a pharmacy, a grocer's at the end of the block. Quickly, she dashed across the square and up the steps of the town hall.

"No one here but us, Callie," Patch called menacingly as he entered the square. Callie hurled herself through the entrance to the town hall and slammed the door behind her.

The ground slid out from under her, and she dropped six feet to a rough landing in the dirt. As she sat up and brushed herself off, she looked up to see that the building was only a false front. It looked solid and real, but in reality it was as false as her hopes of safety were.

"Could have told you, Callie," Patch said as he rounded the far end of the line of buildings. "I've been in Meteor Town lots of times. I know where everything is." He laughed, and the sound rang brutally in Callie's ears. She cupped her hands over them to blot it out, and ran.

The tracks led to a waterfall and disappeared into it. Dead end, Callie thought. She looked back to see Patch closing in on her. She was trapped.

Then she remembered the wall of rock the train had gone through on the tour. If that was an illusion, what was the waterfall? Crossing her fingers, she plunged forward.

The icy water struck her, and she let out a yell of astonishment. Water poured down from sprinkler pipes over the entrance. The waterfall was real enough, another trick to surprise the tourists with.

She slogged out of the water and into the darkness of a tunnel that backed up to the falls. The tracks were almost invisible in the gloom. She tapped them with her foot as she stumbled along. The tracks curved to the left. Callie followed them.

She froze.

Ahead, from a hole in the ceiling, light poured in. The ceiling had collapsed, and rubble, piled from floor to ceiling, covered the tracks and blocked the tunnel. Desperately, Callie dug into the pile, but it was too big. She wouldn't be able to dig a way through before Patch caught up with her, and he barred the way back.

This time, she knew, she was trapped.

"I can't believe Callie would have left this behind," said Joe, holding up the videocassette.

"Not unless she was really in trouble," Frank replied. They hurried to a food stand on the other side of the small lawn. A pretty brunette stood behind the counter. She smiled cheerfully at the Hardys as they approached.

"Good afternoon. Welcome to Meteor Town. What may I get you?" she asked.

"I'll have a hot dog," Joe said.

"Joe!" Frank scowled.

"Well, I'm hungry," Joe said. He turned to the woman, who was putting a hot dog in a bun. "Did you see a young woman come through here recently? About your size and height?"

The girl handed Joe the hot dog and shook her head. "No." She pointed to metal jars on a nearby table. "Catsup, mustard, and relish are over there."

"She might have been with a man wearing a black ninja suit and an eyepatch," Frank added.

"Him I remember. He came tearing through here a few minutes ago. But he was by himself. It was very strange." She flicked a thumb toward a path leading away from the green toward a hilly area. "He went that way."

"Thanks," Frank said.

"You're welcome," the girl called as they headed for the path. "Have a nice day."

They moved warily along the path, Joe eating the hot dog while they trotted. He studied the area. "This opens up in every direction," he said, noting the various sets built in every corner of the valley. "How are we supposed to know where Callie went?"

Frank spied a workman. "Maybe he saw something."

At Frank's questions, the workman bristled. "Nobody's supposed to be here unless they're authorized. Let me see your passes."

"This is an emergency," Frank insisted, and gave the workman Callie's description.

"Yeah, she and some fella with an eyepatch

jumped the gate." The workman glared at the sign. "Can't anyone read anymore?"

"I thought everyone in Meteor Town was cheery," Joe said through his last mouthful of hot dog.

"I don't get paid to deal with the public," the workman snarled.

"Never mind," Frank told Joe. He grabbed his elbow and pulled him toward the gate. "We've got to find Callie."

"Stay out of there!" Undaunted, the Hardys hurdled the gate and sprinted through the field on the other side. "You're in trouble now!" the workman shouted. He turned and stormed off.

"End of the line," Patch taunted. Callie whirled on the mountain of rubble as Patch continued to stalk her, flexing his fingers in a strangling motion. The light from the ceiling reflected a nasty glint in his eye. "It's why they closed this part of the studio. No way out."

There's one way, thought Callie, raising her eyes to the hole in the ceiling. She began climbing up the rubble.

It shifted under her weight, and she slipped back down a few feet. Laughing, Patch grabbed at her. In seconds she had pulled herself to the top of the heap.

Patch began the climb after her. Callie reached

up to the hole in the ceiling, but her fingertips only brushed it.

She crouched low and sprang. Her hands clamped around the edge of the opening, and she held firm and pulled herself up to freedom.

Patch was only a few feet behind her, his arms easily long enough to reach the hole from the top of the pile. Callie spun around, looking for somewhere to hide. She spied a building not too far off and she bolted for it.

Callie slammed the door behind her after she entered the building—that was a mistake. It was pitch-dark inside, and Callie could see nothing. She began feeling her way back to the door, when it opened.

Patch stepped in and switched on the lights.

An alien spaceship appeared to her left, men in armor sitting at the control panels, others were standing guard, futuristic weapons drawn. Robots, she realized. At the far end was an exit, and she ran for it.

Locked.

"Just you and me," Patch muttered in her ear as he pulled her back by her hair. "Callie, we have to have a little talk about a tape." His hand tightened around her throat.

"Let her go!" ordered a male voice from the far door.

"Frank!" Callie cried thankfully as Frank and Joe ran toward them.

Patch laughed viciously, and held Callie for them to see. "Can't stop me," he said. "Looks like I'll have to forget the talk, Callie. This is the end. Sorry, boys, you're too far away to stop me."

"He's right," Joe whispered to Frank. "If we try to rush him—"

Frank eyed the control panels. "Hit every switch you can, Joe! Do it!"

Joe vaulted to one panel and slapped switches on, and Frank did the same. Across the set, robots came to life, their ray guns firing.

"Just lights." Patch laughed. Then a beam hit the wall next to him. The wall burst, showering Patch and Callie with dust and iron filings. Patch screamed in terror, shoved Callie aside, and leapt to a ladder that led to catwalks above the set.

Frank ran to help Callie. "Did he hurt you?"

Callie smiled gratefully. "He was working up to it. Thanks."

Joe joined them. "You sure took a chance, Frank. What if one of those lasers had hit Callie?"

"They weren't lasers," Frank said. "Why would they be? This place is just tricks, remember? I bet some explosive in the wall was set off when the light touched it. Neither of them were in real danger."

Joe looked up at the catwalks. "We've got Patch cornered in here. Let's get him."

Frank nodded and started for the catwalk.

"Hold it!" a new voice shouted. The workman appeared at the door, joined by two security guards, and a tall, good-looking man in an expensive-looking business suit. "That's them."

Despite Callie and the Hardys' protests, the security guards collected them and shoved them back to the door. "We'll throw them off the lot."

"No," said the well-dressed man. He studied them coolly for a moment. Frank and Joe exchanged glances. Who was he?

"Take them to my office," the man said. "And keep them there."

"Yes, sir," the security guard replied. He took Joe roughly by the arm. "Whatever you say—Mr. Bates."

Chapter

14

THE OFFICE WAS enormous, decorated all in leather and mahogany. At one end was a large desk. A painting of Stuart Bates hung on the wall behind it. Two black leather couches faced the desk. Frank and Callie were shoved onto one couch and Joe on the other.

"Sit there and don't touch anything," said one of the guards. They left the brothers and Callie alone.

The office door clicked shut. Instantly, Frank and Joe were on their feet. Joe pressed at the edges of the window, which overlooked all of Meteoric Studios. "No openings here, and we're twelve stories up in any case," he said. "Any luck there?"

Frank wiggled the doorknob. "Locked." He

walked around the room, tapping at the wood paneling on the walls, while Joe slid the painting to one side. "No secret passages in the wall."

"No safe," Joe replied. He let the painting slip back into place. "Anything he's got here must be in his desk."

"What's with you guys?" Callie said. "So we get scolded for trespassing. It's no big deal."

Frank rolled his eyes. "We never told her." He fished the photograph from his pocket. "See that painting on the wall?"

Callie studied it. "Sure."

"Recognize him?" he asked, and handed her the photograph.

Callie paled. "You mean Stuart Bates is—?"

"Looks that way. Whatever you do when he gets here, don't let on that we know," said Joe, who pried uselessly at a desk drawer. "Frank, you still have your credit card?"

Frank handed it to Joe, who bent over and slipped it between a drawer and the desk frame. He wiggled the card until there was a loud click, and the center drawer popped open. With a look of triumph Joe passed the card back.

"Nothing," Joe said as he rifled the desk. The triumphant look faded. "Paper clips, a pen, blank paper." He found a manila file, took it out, and flipped through it. "Company financial records. Nothing out of the ordinary. From his desk you'd think this guy was squeaky clean."

He returned the file and shut the drawer. Keys jingled on the other side of the door. Frank and Joe dove for the couches, and when Stuart Bates came in, they were waiting meekly in their seats.

"We try to run a safe tour here," Bates said in a flat voice as he sat behind his desk. "We can't have people running off on their own no matter how much fun it looks like." He gazed at them impersonally, and for all Frank or Joe could tell, Bates had never seen them before in his life. He had the relaxed, suntanned appearance of a typical Hollywood executive. "I am as much in favor of young people having a good time as anyone else," he said, "but there is simply no excuse for what you did. None."

"You're right," Frank began apologetically.

"Don't blame them," Callie interrupted. "They were saving me."

"From what?" Still the casual but flat, distant tone.

"I was being threatened by a man wearing an eyepatch," Callie said, watching Bates's face. He sat back and gazed at her, almost blank-faced. "He wanted to kill me."

There was still no reaction from Bates. "I hope you're not making this up," he said. Then he shrugged. "I'll tell my men to watch out for such a man." His phone rang. Bates pardoned himself and answered it.

"What'd you say that for?" Frank whispered to Callie.

"Did you see his face?" she whispered back. "He didn't know what I was talking about. He never heard of Patch."

Frank frowned. "Or he's a good actor."

Bates hung up the phone and stood up. "I have an appointment. You'll have to leave the lot immediately, and please don't come back." He opened the office door and signaled Callie and the Hardys out. In the outer office Bates told his secretary, "Call security and have them escorted off the lot." He went back into his office and closed the door.

Frank looked down at the secretary's desk as he passed it. "Distract her for a second," he quietly told Callie.

"Excuse me," Callie asked the secretary, "but is there a—" She paused to glance at Frank and Joe in embarrassment, then leaned close to the secretary and said in hushed tones, "Could we go into the corner? I hate talking about this in front of boys."

The secretary stared at Callie in silence, then abruptly stood and walked to the corner. As her back turned, Frank reached down and slipped a small card and envelope off the desk and into his pocket. In the corner Callie giggled nervously. The secretary flashed her an impatient frown, then marched back to her desk, drew a key from a drawer, and handed it to Callie.

Callie vanished out the office door and returned just in time to meet the security guards, who ushered the three of them to the front gate of the studios. They waited in silence for a bus.

On the bus Callie said, "What was all that about?"

Frank produced the card and read it aloud. " 'You and a guest are invited to a party at the home of Mr. Stuart Bates.' "

"We're going to a party?" Joe said. "Great."

"Callie and I are going," Frank replied. "At least through the front door. You can get in any way you can."

"Frank, we can't go there," said Callie. "He'll recognize us."

"He'll have to see us first. We'll just stay out of his way," Frank explained. "I've got a hunch his house can tell us a lot if we push a little. Joe, do you still have the videotape?"

Joe pulled the cassette from under his shirt and handed it to Frank.

"We're probably barking up the wrong tree," Callie said. "I don't think Bates knew anything. He certainly didn't act guilty."

"Don't forget," said Joe, "nothing's what it looks like in that place. It's all smoke and illusion. Why should Bates be any different?"

"Besides," Frank said, "if Bates doesn't have

any interest in us, what's that man doing here?" He jerked his head toward a man sitting across the aisle and several rows back. The man was short and blond, in his forties, reading a newspaper. He paid no attention to the Hardys.

Callie stole a furtive glance. "I've never seen him before."

"He came out of the studio about the time we got on the bus," Frank said. "He rushed on at the last moment. I think Bates is having him follow us. That's why the security guards took so long to get to the office, to give this guy time to get after us."

"You could be wrong," Joe said. "He looks harmless enough."

"There's an easy way to find out," Frank said. He stood up, and Joe and Callie stood up with him. Together they moved to the front door of the bus.

The short man folded his paper and casually moved to the back door.

The bus stopped and the doors opened. Callie and the Hardys got off in front, and the man got off in back, but at the last moment, Frank, Joe, and Callie climbed back on. The bus pulled away, leaving the short man at the stop, angrily throwing his paper on the ground.

"That answers that question," Frank said as he sat down again. To Callie he said, "Can you duplicate tapes at UCLA?"

"Sure."

"Then that's where we're going," he said, smiling. "It's time to bait a trap for Mr. Stuart Bates."

"Is that all?" asked a young man as he handed Frank two tapes.

"That's it," Callie replied. "Thanks for the duplicating, Dennis. Let me know if I can ever do you a favor."

"Get a bad mark once in a while so we can bring down the class curve," Dennis joked. Laughing at his own words, he walked out, leaving Callie and the Hardys standing alone in the empty lab.

"Yes, this will just about do it," Frank said cheerfully, handing one of the tapes to Callie. She put it in her purse and they walked into the mostly deserted hall. It was dinnertime, and many of the students had gone to eat.

"I could use some supper myself," Joe said, his stomach rumbling. "Then you can tell us all about this great plan of yours." Frank and Joe pushed through a pair of swinging glass doors that led outside.

"No more plans, kids. The game's over," snarled a rough voice behind them as the doors swung shut. Startled, the Hardys spun and slammed into the doors, but it was too late.

Inside, Patch had already locked the door. Joe

and Frank looked back through the glass. In one arm Patch held Callie, his elbow tightly wrapped around her neck. His other hand pressed firmly against her jaw.

"Tape," he yelled through the glass doors, his eyes on the videocassette in Frank's hand. "Trade. The tape, or I break her neck."

"Don't do it, Frank," Callie shouted.

He sharply jerked her head to one side, and Callie screamed as Frank and Joe flinched, expecting to hear the bones in her neck start to crack.

Chapter

15

"STOP!" FRANK SHOUTED through the door. "We'll do whatever you say."

Patch grinned and loosened his grip on Callie, then reached out and flipped the bolt on the doors. "Get in here," he ordered.

Frank and Joe cautiously stepped back into the hall. They looked around. Unfortunately, no one was in sight. "Here's the tape," Frank said, the cassette in his hand. "Let her go."

"Not yet," said Patch. He flagged them back into the lab and to a metal door at the rear of the lab. "Over there." Keeping a tight grip on Callie, he dragged her to the door as the Hardys followed.

"Inside," he said.

Joe opened the door and peered in. The room

116

was filled with shelves, and on each shelf were dozens of round, flat metal boxes. A puff of cool air washed over him. "It's cold in there," he protested.

"In!" Patch demanded, and Joe entered. Frank stepped onto the threshold.

"You promised you wouldn't hurt her."

"Shut up," said Patch. Suddenly his hand snaked out, snatched the cassette from Frank, and shoved Callie into him, knocking them both into the room.

The door slammed shut. Frank and Joe rammed into it, but it wouldn't open.

"What is this place?" Joe wondered aloud.

"The film vault," Callie said. "It's an ongoing project of the school. They track down prints of rare films, restore them, and then make new prints and transfer them to video."

"I remember reading about this stuff," Frank said. He opened a box. Inside was a reel of browning film. "Old film is highly unstable. Something to do with the nitrates in it. Callie, when you say vault, exactly what do you mean?"

"I mean vault. Like in a bank. We're locked in here until someone opens it from outside."

"We're trapped?" Joe asked. He pounded a fist on the door and yelled, "If you can hear us, open up! Help! There are people in here!"

"That won't do any good," Frank said, opening another film can. "No one could hear us. Meanwhile, there might be enough oxygen in here to last till morning. We can't take the chance, and I want to be at Bates's party tonight."

"I don't see that we have any choice," Callie said. "We're stuck here."

"No, we're not," Frank said, opening a third can. "Start going through these and tear off any excess film you can find. Leader footage, projector markers, that kind of thing."

"Great," said Joe. "At least we can stay busy while we're trapped."

"Have some faith," Frank replied. "This place is climate-controlled. I bet they wouldn't like a fire here."

Callie blanched. "I don't like the sound of this, Frank."

"It's simple," he said, tearing off a strip of film. "We burn the film scraps in a can top. There's got to be a fire alarm in a place like this. The fire alarm goes off, someone comes to put out the fire, and we get out."

"Yeah, simple," Joe said, dubious. "I guess it's worth a try."

For several minutes they went through the cans, breaking off whatever blank film they could find, until they had a can filled. "Only one problem," Joe said. "How do we start the fire?"

Frank grinned and turned to Callie. "Nail file."

Callie dug into her purse and brought out a small metal file. Quickly, Frank worked on the screws on the light switch next to the door, until the switch plate came free from the wall. He pulled the wiring from the switch and touched two wires together in the film can. The film burst into flames.

"I don't hear any alarm," Joe said.

Moments later Callie noticed a strange sensation. She realized the air in the room was rushing upward. "Frank! It feels like a vacuum cleaner's loose in here." Then she knew. "There's no alarm. They have a built-in vacuum that puts out fires by drawing all the oxygen out of the vault."

She gagged. "I can't breathe."

Callie sprawled against a shelf, and the Hardys collapsed against her.

This is it, Joe thought as he rolled over on the floor. I never thought it would end this way.

The struggle to breathe was so hard they didn't hear the door quietly click, and didn't realize it had opened until they felt the welcome rush of warm, fresh air. Greedily, they gulped oxygen until they were able to talk again.

"What happened?" Joe asked as they crawled out into the spacious, empty lab. The fire in the vault had gone out completely.

"It must be one of those fail-safe systems," said Frank. "In case anyone was trapped in there during a fire, they'd be able to get out as soon as the danger was over.''

"I don't care how we got out," Callie said. "I'm just glad we did."

"You feel like doing some shopping?" Frank asked her.

"Shopping?" Joe and Callie said together, astonished.

"To get some nice clothes," Frank said. "We have a party to go to."

Bel Air lay north of UCLA and west of Beverly Hills. Among the wealthy in Los Angeles, it was *the* place to have a home. To enter Bel Air, cars had to pass through gates.

Stuart Bates's house was a mansion, a sprawling three stories high with more than two dozen rooms. To one side of the house was a swimming pool and tennis court, and to the other side a smaller pool.

The whole estate was nestled in woods at the north end of one of the canyon roads and was surrounded on three sides by a man-made stream that looked like a moat. It was a home fit for a king of Hollywood, and Stuart Bates, as head of Meteoric Studios, could certainly lay claim to the crown.

Only one bridge led over the stream. And at the entrance to the bridge a man built like a moose checked invitations. No one would get into the Bates party uninvited.

Callie and the Hardys were dropped off by a cab and walked down the road, awed by the line of limousines waiting to get onto the grounds. Frank wore a tuxedo, and Callie had on a deep purple strapless evening dress with a gold sash around the waist. Joe was more casually dressed, in a tan suit and a tie.

"This is hopeless," Callie said finally. "If we *walk* up, they'll know something's wrong. We should have hired a limo."

Frank was thinking. "You're on your own," he told Joe. Then he took Callie by the arm and walked up to a waiting limousine.

"I say." Frank put on a slight British accent as the passengers in the car rolled down their window. "We've had a spot of trouble. Our limo broke down half a mile back, and it's such bad form to enter on foot. Might we . . . ?" He trailed off, flashing the men inside the car his friendliest smile.

"Sure," one of them said, and opened the car door. Frank and Callie climbed in. "I saw you in a film last winter, didn't I?"

Frank lowered his eyes modestly. "I did star in a couple of teen flicks," he lied. "But tonight I'm traveling incognito, if you know what I mean." The others laughed and winked at Callie. Joe ducked among the trees as the cars slowly rolled by, and looked for an opening. He had to get past Bates's security, but how? He studied the passing cars, keeping an eye out for an unlatched trunk or an open door. Nothing. If I'm going to do it, he decided, I'll have to do it by myself.

Sticking to the trees that lined the drive, he walked along the line of cars up to the moat. Then he turned to the right and followed the moat, still protected by the dense forest.

Joe's hunch was right. The moat didn't go all the way around the estate. Bates probably assumed that the thicket of woods would discourage most people from trying to get in that way. But no woods were thick enough to keep Joe Hardy out. Neither was the fence that just appeared in front of him.

Whistling casually, Joe easily topped the fence and strolled through the trees and onto Bates's estate.

He had taken five steps, when a low growl sounded to his left. Before he could react, there was another growl to his right. He came to a full stop, trying not even to breathe.

Two huge Dobermans came bounding toward him, their growls becoming lower and more menacing. Joe had seen dogs like this before, killers trained to attack the slightest movement. Their strong jaws could tear a grown man apart in seconds. And they were the Bates estate's last line of defense. Joe knew that one twitch, one sign of weakness, and the Dobermans would be on him.

The two dogs tensed, baring long razor-sharp teeth, waiting for Joe to make a move, any move.

Chapter

16

JOE CLOSED HIS EYES and tried to figure the distance to the woods behind him. If he could reach the trees before the dogs got him, he could climb to safety, out of their reach. But the growling grew more ominous. Joe knew he'd never make it in time. His muscles were starting to feel the strain of remaining rigid. He wondered how hard it was to knock out a dog, and if he could take out one before the other reached him.

A whistle broke the silence. The dogs turned and streaked to a man who had suddenly appeared nearby. Joe couldn't remember being happier to see anyone in his life, although, like the moose checking invitations at the bridge, this man wore the crimson blazer of Bates's private security force.

The man fastened leashes to the dogs. They tugged at the leads and snapped at Joe, but the man held them safely back.

"What are you doing here?" the man demanded coldly.

"The party," Joe said. He waved vaguely toward the house. "Too noisy. I came out here for some air and quiet."

"Good reflexes," the man said with a hint of admiration. "You're lucky you're still alive. That's why Mr. Bates doesn't want his guests wandering the grounds. You must be new, or you'd know that."

"Yeah, this is my first party here," Joe replied, sounding contrite. "I'll know better next time." He began to walk away.

The man watched him suspiciously. "Hold it!" he said. "Let's see your invitation."

What now? Joe thought, and looked at the dogs. If he knocked out the security guard, the dogs would be free again, and this time he doubted that he'd survive. He decided to bluff it out. "I left it in the house. I didn't know you needed it all the time."

"You don't know much, do you, buddy?" the guard said. "Let's go see your invite."

Closely followed by the man and the dogs, Joe started the long walk to the house.

* * *

Arm in arm, Frank and Callie entered Stuart Bates's home.

It was filled with hundreds of guests. Waiters in white jackets and gloves moved throughout the crowd, carrying trays of food and champagne. The floors were made of polished marble. Priceless paintings covered the walls.

"That looks like real gold leaf on those frames," Callie said to Frank as they stopped to admire the paintings.

Frank watched an actress go by. "That's—" he began, and then his eye was caught by a passing talk-show host. "And that's—"

Callie nudged him nervously. "Don't gawk. We have to act like we fit in, or our cover will be blown." A man brushed past her, and she turned toward him and gasped. He stood almost seven feet tall, with muscles that strained the seams of his dinner jacket.

"Oh, gosh," she said breathlessly. "That's that famous bodybuilder. What's his name? I've got to get his autograph."

Frank took her by the arm and dragged her into the next room. It was a library, lined floor to ceiling with books. There were fewer people in there, and they spoke quietly among themselves, paying no attention to Frank and Callie. "It's hard to keep from being awed, isn't it?" he asked Callie. "I guess everyone who's anyone in this town is here."

"Bates is a powerful man in the entertainment industry, that's for sure," Callie said. There was a round of applause in the other room, and a tall, handsome, smiling man stepped into view. "Uh-oh. There's Bates."

"This way," Frank said, and took her hand. A glass door led from the library onto a terrace at the back of the house, where dance music throbbed. Frank and Callie danced their way through the crowd until they came to another door, and quietly slipped into the kitchen, where chefs and waiters were scrambling to fill trays with appetizers.

Before they were seen, they darted out into the hall. A stairway led up to the second floor, but it had been roped off at the bottom. "Come on," Frank hissed, unfastening the velvet rope. "I want to know why the second floor's off limits." Quickly, Callie followed him up the stairs.

One by one they tried the doors along the main corridor. "Everything's empty," Callie exclaimed. "There's not a stick of furniture in any of these rooms."

"I guess he doesn't use them if he lives here alone," said Frank. "But where's his bedroom?" As they passed a marble stairway that led downstairs, a security guard unfastened the rope blocking it off and started up.

Frank and Callie ducked into an empty room. Keeping the door open a crack, they watched the guard go by. Then they slid off their shoes and slipped soundlessly out after him.

The guard walked to the end of the hall and up a set of stairs to the third floor. He swung open two brass-handled doors and disappeared into a room. Stepping into the room across the hall, Frank and Callie listened as the guard left the room and closed the door. His footsteps echoed down the hall and then down the stairs. When there was no more sound, Frank peeked into the hall.

"No sign of anyone. Let's check out that room."

After they stole through the brass-handled doors, Callie's jaw dropped.

The room was huge. A king-size bed with oak posts and silk covers was centered on one wall. Around the room she saw a projection television with a videodisc player and several videocassette recorders, a full stereo, a wet bar, and an exercise area complete with bodybuilding equipment. At one end another door led into an extravagant bathroom.

"There's a hot tub in here!" Callie said. "And it's filled with bubbly steaming water." On a shelf at the edge of the tub was a cordless telephone. Callie imagined Bates sitting in the tub, using the phone to make multimillion-dollar deals.

"The man who has everything," Frank said.

He took the photograph they had gotten from Patch out of his pocket. "I need the tape now."

Callie took the videocassette from her purse and handed it to him. He laid the photo and the cassette on top of Bates's pillow.

"That ought to shake him up," Frank said with a chuckle.

"Frank, come here," Callie cried. While he had been baiting the trap, she looked at Bates's closets. As Frank faced her, she pulled out a carefully folded patrolman's outfit from the far corner behind rows of expensive suits.

"Ah-ha," Frank said. "Just what we were looking for."

"There are running shoes in back too." Callie picked them up, then brushed off her hands. "They're covered with sand."

"It wouldn't hold up as evidence in front of a jury," Frank said, "but it convinces me. Bates is our man all right."

Footsteps reverberated on the floor outside. "Someone's coming. Hide!" Callie said, and shut herself in the closet.

"Not in the closet!" Frank whispered urgently. "They might look there."

She came out as the footsteps neared. "Where?"

Frank looked around frantically. There was nowhere to hide. "Under the bed," he ordered. She dropped to the floor and disappeared.

The door began to open.

Quickly, Frank dived across the room, sliding into the bathroom. He closed the door just as Bates and a guard came into the bedroom.

Through the door Frank heard Bates and the guard talk animatedly. He made out words about time and a phone call. Suddenly they stopped.

After an electrified silence Bates said, "Someone's been here. Search the place."

The voices were headed for the bathroom. Frank had scant seconds before he'd be caught. There was only one thing to do.

The guard opened the bathroom door and looked around. "No one here," he said, and left, shutting the door.

Frank rose up out of the hot tub, dripping wet. He took a towel from a nearby rack and began to quietly dry himself. The water ran silently down his back and legs and onto the marble floor. He'd have to mop up.

The phone rang.

Cautiously, Frank moved closer to the bathroom door and listened until the ringing stopped and Bates's voice was heard again. Then Frank gently lifted the cordless phone from its cradle and put it to his ear.

A gruff-voiced man was on the line, arguing with Bates. "No more excuses, Stuart," the voice was saying. "You double-crossed me once with the bank. You're not going to trick me again.''

Frank held his breath, glued to the phone. The gruff-voiced caller must be Patch!

Fascinated, Frank listened while the two argued over who had betrayed whom. The entire picture of the robbery unfolded for Frank.

Apparently, Bates and Moran—Patch—had thought that the highway patrol had identified Moran as he fled. Bates talked Moran into helping him knock off a buddy with a firebomb and switching dental records so the body would be identified as Moran. They placed a few carefully charred bills from the robbery on the vagrant's body to fool the police into thinking they'd found one of the thieves. Moran, believed dead, was free. But before Moran realized what was happening, Bates had vanished, taking all the money.

"Too bad I ran across your picture in the paper," Patch said angrily. "Too bad for you."

"All right. What now?" Bates asked brusquely.

"We meet again. In a crowded place. Tomorrow. And this time I take the whole two million." Patch paused for emphasis. "I have a videotape now. I'll send it to the police."

As Frank listened, his nose began to itch. He rubbed it, but the itching wouldn't stop.

Suddenly Frank sneezed.

All talking on the phone stopped. The bathroom door flew open. The guard stood there, gun in hand, and waved Frank into the bedroom.

"You!" Bates said, his face mottled red with fury. All trace of the urbane executive was gone from him now. "Take him out back," he told the guard. "*Way* back. And do what you have to."

As the guard yanked Frank's arms tighter behind him, making him cry out in pain, Callie continued to lie silently under the bed. She didn't dare move, aware that all she could do now was listen.

"No, there's no problem," Bates snapped into the phone. "Everything's under control. Where do we meet, and when?" Callie tried to make out the answer, but she knew it was hopeless. The voice on the other end of the line was inaudible to her. "Fine. I'll be there," Bates said. There was the click of the phone being hung up.

"Well?" she heard Bates ask the guard. "What are you waiting for? Get him out of here."

She twisted for a better view, propping up the edge of the bedspread so she could see out from under it. Three sets of feet were in view, one set tapping impatiently. Someone came around the bed in wet stocking feet. Frank, she realized. Like her, he had never put his shoes back on. She gripped her high heels and waited for the next pair of feet to pass.

When a shoe came into view, she stuck out one

of her high heels, catching the guard's ankle and tripping him. He cried out in surprise as he fell.

Frank spun abruptly at the cry. Arm straight, he smashed the back of his hand into the guard's neck. The impact knocked the guard off his feet, but his finger tightened around the trigger of his gun. Frank smashed his elbow into the guard's chest.

The gun went off as the guard jerked from the impact of the blow. The bullet slammed into a bedpost. The guard lay silent, unconscious. Startled, Bates ducked into his closet.

"Get out from under there," Frank said, giving Callie a helping hand.

"What happened to Bates?" she whispered as she stood up.

Frank pointed to the closet for reply. They walked over to it and pulled open the doors. Bates waited there, hunched over, his back turned toward them. "Come on, Bates. It's over."

"It is," Bates agreed. Then he turned around and stood, hatred and victory in his eyes. In one hand he held the holster he had worn with the patrolman's uniform. In his other hand he held the gun. "It's over for you."

Chapter

17

"I'VE GOT TO FIND my brother," Joe told the guard as they neared the mansion. "He's got our invitations." The guard motioned Joe on as he tied the dogs to a post. Then he caught up with him, and they approached the terrace from the surrounding trees. Joe pointed to the dance floor. "Oh, look. There he is."

The guard turned his head, and Joe jabbed a fist into his stomach. He swung back, and Joe jumped away from his fist and landed a haymaker on his jaw. Unnoticed by the dancers, the guard crumpled to the ground.

Joe ran inside the house, looking for Frank and Callie. But there were too many people for him to see anyone.

He heard a gunshot above.

"Frank," he shouted, dashing to the stairs.

"You can't go up there," a guard said, standing at the roped-off bottom step. Without a word Joe ducked under the rope and streaked up the stairs two at a time, the guard hot on his heels.

Joe heard no voices on the second floor and dashed on to the third.

There he came to a door with brass handles. He heard Bates's voice saying "It's over for you" as he slammed open the door and dove into the room.

Shocked at the intrusion, Bates spun and started to fire. Joe cried out, but before Bates could pull the trigger, Frank grabbed his gun hand, twisting himself under Bates's arm, and drove his elbow into Bates's shoulder, exactly as his karate teacher had taught him. Bates fell back, the gun slipping from his hand.

"You're all wet, Frank," Joe said, having taken care of the guard who had followed him. "What happened, did Callie finally get fed up and throw you in the pool?"

"Very funny. Wait here while I change." Frank picked up the pistol, handed it to Joe, and left him to guard Bates and the two security men while he went over to inspect the clothes in the closet. "What do you think?" he asked Joe and Callie. "A summer wool?"

"The blue would look nice on you." Callie grinned.

"The blue it is," Frank said, pulling the expensive suit out with a flourish and choosing a shirt and socks from the shelves. "Be back in a minute." With a nod to the glowering Bates, Frank disappeared into the bathroom to change.

"Let's get out of here," he said when he reappeared, looking elegant in the expensive suit. He took the gun from Joe, walked back to the bathroom door, and tossed it into the hot tub.

"What about him?" Joe asked. They looked at Bates, who sat on the floor, angrily clutching his hurt shoulder.

"We can't kidnap him," Frank said. "We'd never get out of here. It'd be better going after Patch. Bates'll be here later." He glanced at Bates. "We'd better leave before he and his guards recover enough to attack us."

As they headed for the door, Frank lifted the videocassette from the pillow on the bed and handed it to Callie. Then they hurried down the stairs and out the back door. "This way," said Joe, who lead them past the dogs toward the woods. The Dobermans strained their leashes and barked loudly as the three teens passed. "They'll be expecting us to leave the front way, not through here."

Callie saw the cassette in Frank's hand. "I thought leaving that was part of your trap."

"We don't need it now," Frank said. "Bates has trapped himself, and so has Patch, or whatever he's called. They're meeting tomorrow for the big payoff, and I think we should be there."

Just as the three had made it safely to the fence at the edge of Bates's property, Callie stopped suddenly. "Wait," she said to Frank and Joe. "Do you hear something—like an animal?"

Frank and Joe held their breath. Now they heard it too. A baying, like wolves closing in on their prey.

"The Dobermans!" Joe yelled. "Bates must have alerted the guards. They're coming closer!"

In one movement the three ran for the fence as the baying Dobermans came closer. "You first, Callie," Frank ordered. He and Joe boosted her up, and as she grabbed the top of the fence, they climbed up after her.

The baying grew closer. Just as the boys topped the fence they saw the Dobermans break free of the trees and leap toward them. Behind them ran two guards with guns.

"Jump!" said Joe. The Hardys and Callie dropped down on the other side of the fence and ran for safety. Behind them the dogs howled in frustration and bullets pinged in the air.

"Now what?" asked Joe as they stopped, panting.

"Bates and Patch are meeting tomorrow for the payoff," Frank answered, trying to catch his breath. "I think we should be there."

"Great," said Joe. "Where's the meet?"

"Don't know that."

"That's wonderful," Joe said, disgusted. "How are we supposed to find out? The only people who know are Bates and Moran."

"Bates will be looking for us," Callie added. "Patch could be anywhere in the city. The meeting could be anywhere."

"True," Frank said. "Callie, would your friends be willing to help us?"

"I think so," answered Callie. "Help us do what?"

"Isn't it obvious?" Frank said. "We're going to find and follow Patch."

"Everyone in place?" Frank asked. He checked his watch. It was ten o'clock. Rested and showered and eating breakfast at a sidewalk café in Westwood, Frank felt ready for anything.

"You sure this is going to work?" Joe said. He checked his own watch. "Trusting street people is kind of chancy."

"Not really." Frank bit into a slice of bacon. "With years of surviving on the street, Patch must have developed certain habits. His habits will trip him up now."

"The street people know all the places he hangs out, Joe," Callie explained. At her feet was equipment borrowed from the university, a video camera and a portable power pack. "They're checking out each place for us. If Patch shows up, they'll spot him, and they'll call and tell us where he is."

"All I overheard," Frank said, "is that Patch wants to meet in a public place."

"After the last so-called payoff, he probably won't want to meet Bates at night," continued Callie.

"So it'll probably be this morning or this afternoon," Joe said, "if we haven't read him all wrong."

"I hope we haven't," Callie reminded them. "I called Aunt Emma from the hotel this morning. She said she was going to call the police if I'm not home by ten tonight." She grinned at Frank. "She thinks you guys are a bad influence on me."

"You got us into this," Joe protested, but he saw that Callie was laughing.

The wait at the café was a long one. Callie and the Hardys had to order half a dozen refills of coffee just to keep their table. Finally, two and a half hours later, a waiter came to their table. "Phone call for Callie Shaw."

"I'll take it," Callie said, and followed the waiter to the phone inside the restaurant. Two minutes later she returned.

"That was Adrienne. She found Patch on Venice Beach. We're in luck. The meeting is in Westwood."

Joe looked uncertain. "How does she know?"

"She followed him."

139

At that, Frank frowned. "She shouldn't have done that. Moran's dangerous."

"Don't worry," Callie said. "He didn't see her. He seemed to be concerned with getting to the first showing at the Westwood Tower Cinema."

Joe snapped his fingers. "I know that place. It's right down the street." He stood up, dug money from his pockets to pay for the food, and dropped it on the table. "We've got to get there before the payoff goes down."

They hurried through the crowded Westwood streets until the spire of the Tower Cinema came into sight.

Patch was clever, Joe thought. The place was empty enough for an exchange to go unnoticed, but crowded enough to keep Bates from getting cute.

And empty enough for us to get a good view of the whole thing, he reminded himself. He laughed. Patch's cleverness would provide the evidence against him.

"Three, please," Frank said at the ticket booth, handing the man in the window several bills. The ticket seller slid three tickets to him along with the change. Callie and the Hardys walked into the theater.

It wasn't until the man at the door took his ticket that Joe felt suspicious. Something was wrong, and he racked his brains to figure out what it was. Nothing came to mind. The whole thing was what anyone would expect from an afternoon at the movies.

The smell, he realized. He caught the strong odor of mothballs in the air. It seemed to come from the clothes the moviegoers around him were wearing—the moviegoers, the ticket taker, everyone. As though the clothes had been in storage—in a costume wardrobe. Joe looked quickly around him. Now he realized something else. All of the people were men!

He looked back to see the entrance to the theater being locked shut.

"Split!" he yelled to Frank and Callie. "It's a trap!"

Something hard smacked across the back of his head, and Joe tumbled into blackness. When he woke, he was on the floor in front of the first row of theater seats, the big screen looming beside him. With him were Frank and Callie, and next to Callie was Patch. They all had their arms tied behind their backs. As Joe tried to stand, he realized his arms were tied too. A strong hand lifted him to his feet, and he saw all the moviegoers around him, their guns aimed at him.

Like a conquering hero, Bates stepped to the center of the narrow movie-theater stage.

"Funny seeing you here," Joe said.

141

"Nothing funny about it, hero," replied Bates. "In fact, it's a downright tragedy."

He dropped down from the stage and shoved the nose of a revolver under Joe's chin. "And in case I need to remind you, pal, in a tragedy the hero always dies."

Chapter

18

"HOW DID YOU KNOW we were coming?" Frank asked grimly.

Bates chuckled. "Of *course* you were going to find out where Moran and I were meeting. I never doubted it."

Patch glared at him.

"I couldn't have done it without Moran," Bates continued. "It was his idea to meet here. Lots of people around." He picked up a briefcase from a seat and opened it. Inside were packets of one-hundred-dollar bills. "I even made it look real for him.

"But I have a lot of connections in this town, and my money talks. It wasn't hard to rent this theater for a private screening this afternoon."

"Does that mean we get to see the main feature before we go?" Joe quipped.

Bates grinned with half his mouth and tousled Joe's hair. "You *are* the main feature, buddy boy. I've got the tapes. Thanks for remembering your copy, Callie. I've got Moran, I've got you. You're the only other people who know what's going on, so you've got to go." He gestured to his men to close in. "We're going to take you a long, long way from here, and you're just going to disappear."

"You can't get away with it," Callie cried. "If you take us out on the street, we'll scream."

"Sweetie, I bought my way into legitimacy and power, and I can get away with anything," Bates snapped back. "You're not going on the street. There's a van out back. We're taking you out in that, far from any prying eyes."

"What if we don't want to go?" Frank said, a threatening tone in his voice. "You'll have to kill us here, and that'll be messy. It would be traced to you."

"Let me put it this way. If you give me even the slightest bit of trouble"—Bates nodded toward Callie—"she'll die first. Got it? Now, let's go."

Bound and surrounded by Bates's armed men, the Hardys, Callie, and Patch were led up a long ramp into the back of the theater. There, a bay door swung open, and Frank and Joe saw the blue van, its windows opaqued, sitting directly outside, parked in a driveway.

They stepped into the driveway, and Frank looked to the street. Too far away to make a run for it, he decided, and he knew what would happen to Callie if he did. There was no one else around, no one to see Bates take them away.

Bates's thugs began forcing the captives into the van one by one. "Work on the ropes," Frank whispered to Joe as he fell on the floor beside him. "Mine are starting to loosen. Watch for any chance."

"Way ahead of you, brother," Joe whispered back.

"Shut up in there," Bates said as he shoved Patch in. He squeezed Callie's shoulder and muscled her toward the door.

Before he could get Callie into the van, though, a teenage boy appeared at the mouth of the driveway. His face was dirty, and his dark hair shaggy and jumbled. His old blue jeans were torn at the knees, and the soles of his shoes flopped loose as he walked. When he saw Bates, he beamed and stretched out his hand. "Spare change?"

Before Bates could react, a badly dressed, unshaven black man entered the driveway, heading toward Bates. "Spare change?"

"Go away. Beat it," said Bates. He waved the gun at them threateningly, but they kept coming. Angrily, he pulled a handful of coins from his pocket and threw them at the panhandlers. The coins struck the driveway and rolled, and the panhandlers dropped to their knees and scooped them up.

The guards and Bates were distracted for an instant by this behavior, and that instant was all Callie needed to make her move. She kicked Bates hard in the shin. With a yell he let her go, and she began to run. Before she was halfway down the driveway, Bates took careful aim at her back.

"Spare change?" called a third voice as a woman wandered into the driveway. And another voice and another and another. Callie's eyes widened.

It was Adrienne and the rest of the street people.

Bates lowered his gun as the mob flooded the driveway. There was no way to pick Callie out of this crowd. At least the Hardys and Patch were still in the van, though, he decided. "Get in," Bates ordered his men. "Drive out of here. Run over anyone you have to." He tossed the briefcase and the videocassettes into the back of the van, and started to climb in.

Joe, his hands still tied, threw himself forward from the back of the van like a cannonball, whacking Bates in the stomach with his shoulder and knocking the gun out of his hand. Bates's men, still outside the van, pointed their guns at

Joe's back, but before they could shoot, Frank kicked the other van door hard. It swung around, ramming into one of Bates's men and causing the two with the guns on Joe to spin toward Frank. With a piercing yell Frank leapt high in the air. His feet lashed out, catching the men hard in their jaws. They fell back, unconscious.

Meanwhile, Bates had gotten Joe pinned against the van and was strangling him. Joe twisted in Bates's grip, but with his hands behind his back, he had no leverage. He couldn't break Bates's hold.

With his last shred of energy Joe stabbed his head forward, cracking his forehead into Bates. Stunned, the movie executive let go and stumbled away. By now the driveway was full of street people. They ran at once and seized Bates and his men and held them down.

"That about wraps that up," said Joe as Callie untied his hands.

Frank pulled his wrists free, and the ropes fell away. Bates was defeated, and with satisfaction Frank saw the street people had everything under control. Except for one thing, he abruptly realized.

The briefcase carrying the two million dollars was gone, and so was Patch.

"Callie!" he shouted. "Take charge here." To Joe he said, "We're one short on the head count." They raced to the street.

Patch, the briefcase in his hands, which were still tied behind his back, had just turned the corner at the end of the block and disappeared.

"There he is!" Joe yelled as they rounded the corner a few seconds later. Patch was having trouble holding on to the briefcase and running through the Westwood crowds at the same time. The Hardys could hear shouts of surprise as Patch bumped into pedestrians, knocking them aside. Step by step, they were catching up to the thief.

Patch twirled as they neared him, and shouldered a woman into the Hardys' way. Joe tripped and tumbled, and Patch cast himself into the heavy traffic in the street. If he could make it to the other side, Frank knew, they'd have an even harder time catching him.

Tires screamed, and Patch stood frozen in fear as a delivery truck careened toward him. Frank dove at him, tackling him, hoping against hope there would be time to get out of the way of the onrushing truck. But as he rolled, it seemed time had run out.

The squeal of brakes ended, followed by a sickening thud.

Sprawled against a parked car, with Patch lying dazed at his side, Frank stared at the open briefcase crushed by the truck's front tire. The money was scattering across the street, blown by the wind. That had stopped traffic as nothing else could.

Patch struggled to get to the money, but Frank held him pinned against the parked car. Joe came over to them, a bundle of money in his hand. "Looking for this?" he asked, thumbing the bills in Patch's face.

The top bill was real money, but everything underneath was cut from old newspaper clippings.

"Looks like Bates conned you, Moran," Frank said. "You both conned each other right into prison."

Moran spat. "So what if Bates and I stole that money?" he finally said. "So what if I killed some guy years ago? I'll never admit that to anyone else. Do you really think the cops will believe a famous producer and an old bum are partners in crime? They'll laugh you all the way back to wherever you came from."

"No more of the harmless street artist act, Moran," Joe said. He grasped Patch by the collar and raised a fist. "You'll tell everything, or—"

"Or what?" Moran sneered. "You'll beat a poor old drifter up?"

"They don't have to," said a familiar voice. The Hardys looked up to see Callie there, her videocamera recording everything Patch had said.

"I got the whole thing on tape," Callie said. "I have my story."

Joe waited impatiently in the boarding line at Los Angeles International Airport as Frank said goodbye to Callie. Emma Beaudry watched from nearby.

"Thanks for all your help," Callie told Frank.

"My pleasure, Callie. Anything for you, you know that." He looked into her eyes. "The funny thing was that the statute of limitations on that robbery ran out long ago. If they hadn't killed anyone, they could have walked away with the whole thing."

Callie nodded. "Still, it was nice of the armored car company to award a finder's fee for the money."

"And it was nice of you to donate it to your street friends," Frank said. "It'll go a long way toward helping them."

"Well, they did save our lives," said Callie. A sad look came over Callie's face. "It's too bad you can't stay until I finish my course. You'll call me, won't you?"

Frank gently hugged her. "Callie, of course I'll call. And I'll see you when you get back."

"I can't believe you guys," Emma remarked, shaking her head in bewilderment. "When I was Callie's age, we'd have a burger and maybe catch a flick at the drive-in. You two seem to think romance means throwing a couple of lowlifes in jail."

"Don't judge me by those two, Emma," Joe said, affecting a serious scowl. "Anytime you want a burger and a movie, Joe Hardy's your man."

"Well, at least there's one gentleman left in Los Angeles." Emma laughed, giving Joe a kiss on the cheek.

Callie smiled through the tears welling up in her eyes. "Your plane's about to leave," she said to Frank. "You'd better get going."

They hugged again, and then Frank went to join Joe in line. At the gate he waved back to Callie. "Good-bye!"

"So long," she called back. Joe and Emma also waved goodbye, exchanging grins. Then the brothers marched up the long passage, and in a few minutes they were seated on the plane.

"You know," Joe said, "it's funny."

"What is?" Frank asked.

"It's all turned around. Usually when we go home, *I'm* the one who has to leave the girl behind."

Frank and Joe's next case:

While trying to help Annie Shea, the pretty new girl in town, Joe accidentally runs down her old boyfriend, Phil. Joe's in a tight spot, but Annie seems afraid to help. Then the Hardys learn that Phil is the prime suspect in a million-dollar diamond robbery and Annie may be involved.

But when Annie is kidnapped, the brother detectives swing into action. They follow her to the lair of America's most infamous gem thief, Cutter. Outnumbered, the Hardys take on the diamond man's gang in an all-out effort to save Annie—and clear Joe of murder . . . in *Witness to Murder*, Case #20 in The Hardy Boys Casefiles™.